Lost in Rome

Also by Cindy Callaghan

Just Add Magic

Lost in London

Lost in Paris

Coming Soon

Lost in Ireland

(Previously titled *Lucky Me*)

Lost in Rome

CINDY CALLAGHAN

Aladdin
New York   London   Toronto   Sydney   New Delhi

ALADDIN

An imprint of Simon & Schuster Children's Publishing Division
1230 Avenue of the Americas, New York, NY 10020
This Aladdin hardcover edition August 2015
Text copyright © 2015 by Cindy Callaghan
Jacket illustration copyright © 2015 by Annabelle Metayer
Also available in an Aladdin M!X paperback edition.
All rights reserved, including the right of reproduction in whole or
in part in any form.
ALADDIN is a trademark of Simon & Schuster, Inc.,
and related logo is a registered trademark of Simon & Schuster, Inc.
For information about special discounts for bulk purchases,
please contact Simon & Schuster Special Sales at 1-866-506-1949 or
business@simonandschuster.com.
The Simon & Schuster Speakers Bureau can bring authors to your live event.
For more information or to book an event contact the
Simon & Schuster Speakers Bureau at 1-866-248-3049 or
visit our website at www.simonspeakers.com.
Jacket designed by Jessica Handelman
Interior designed by Hilary Zarycky
The text of this book was set in Berkeley Oldstyle.
Manufactured in the United States of America 0715 FFG
2 4 6 8 10 9 7 5 3 1
Library of Congress Control Number 2014950428
ISBN 978-1-4814-4282-4 (hc)
ISBN 978-1-4814-2603-9 (pbk)
ISBN 978-1-4814-2604-6 (eBook)

This is a book about sisters, so this is for Sue as well as all my other special gal pals whom I consider sisters. In the pizza of life, sisters are the pepperoni.

Acknowledgments

Writers often ask me for advice, and I always tell them to find trusted partners. I'm lucky to have this in Gale, Carolee, Josette, Jane, Chris, and Shannon, and the Northern Delaware Sisters in Crime group: John, KB, Jane, June, Chris, Janis, Susan, and Kathleen.

Thanks to my friends, who understand that I talk to imaginary people and are fine with it.

Mille grazie to my literary agent, Mandy Hubbard, and editor, Alyson Heller. Sometimes we're so like-minded that it gets scary.

As always, to my family: Ellie, Evan, Happy, Kevin, my parents, nieces and nephews, sister, sisters-in-law, brothers-in-law, and mother-in-law, thank you for your continued encouragement! Special thanks to my niece Taylor and daughter, Happy, who for the low, low price of a diner breakfast helped me plot out a Summer Rome-ance with Extra Cheese.

Also a *grazie* goes out to my helpful translators: Shari, Eddi, and Vic.

To teachers, librarians, and, most of all, my readers: I love getting your e-mails, letters, pictures, selfies, posts, and tweets. . . . Keep 'em coming!

1

I'd been planning to be a counselor-in-training at Camp Hiawatha, but there was an issue with fleas, mice, lice, and snakes and the camp closing, leaving my summer *wide open*.

The only question was, what would I do with all my free time? Thankfully, my parents were able to make alternate plans.

"It's all set," my mom said.

"For real?" I asked.

"Totally for real," Dad confirmed. "Your great-aunt Maria can't wait to have you."

My great-aunt Maria was my dad's aunt, and she was more than *great*, she was my favorite relative in the adult category. She was sweet, nice, an amazing Italian cook, and she owned this insanely cute pizzeria. Plus, I always felt like she and I had some kind of special connection—like a bond or something. I can't explain it exactly.

Oh, and that pizzeria she owned? It just happened to be in Rome. Rome, Italy!

Basically, Aunt Maria is all that and a plate of rigatoni, if you know what I mean.

"When do we leave?" I asked.

"Tomorrow morning," Mom said. "But this isn't going to be two weeks of sightseeing and touristy stuff. I told her you wanted to work."

"At the pizzeria?"

"Yeah," Dad said. "She's planning to teach you how to make her signature sauce."

"The secret sauce?" I asked in awe.

"That's the one," he added. "*I* don't even know how to make it."

"That's a major deal," Mom said.

Just then a girl who looked a lot like me—long dark curly hair, light skin, brown eyes, except she was taller, prettier, older, and more stylish—walked into our parents' room, where we were talking. A cell phone was glued to her ear.

"It's on!" I said.

"For real?" she asked.

"For real!"

She pumped her fist in the air. "I'll call you later. I'm going to Rome! *Ciao!*" She hung up the phone, looked at herself in the full-length mirror, fluffed her brown curly locks, and practiced, *"Buongiorno!"*

Maybe I should tell you who "she" is: my older sister, Gianna. She's like my best friend. There's no one I'd rather be with for two weeks in Rome. Next year she'll be a junior in high school, where she is most often seen with a glitter pen and scrapbooking scissors.

Me . . . not so much. I'm more of a big-idea gal. Then she builds or glues or sews or staples my ideas into reality.

This fall she'll start looking at colleges. She's excited about it, but the idea of her leaving home makes my stomach feel like a lump of overcooked capellini. Maybe some sisters fight, but Gi and I are tight. (Okay, *sometimes* we fight like sisters.)

Mom said to Gianna, "I told Lucy that you girls are going to work at the pizzeria."

"I love that place," Gianna said. "I hope it's exactly the same as I remember it."

"Do you think she still has Meataball?" I asked. I had visited Aunt Maria and her pizzeria years ago, and I vaguely remembered her cat.

"The cat?" Dad asked. "He has to be dead by now, honey. But maybe she has another cat."

"Gi, she's gonna teach me how to make her sauce."

"Just you?"

I shrugged. "Maybe she loves me more."

Mom said, "No. She loves you both exactly the same."

"Maybe," I started, "she wants me to take over the pizzeria when she retires, and I'll be the Sauce Master, the only one in the entire Rossi lineage who knows the ancient family signature sauce. Then, when I'm old, I'll choose one of my great-nieces to carry on the family tradition. And—"

Mom interrupted. "Lucy?"

"What?"

"This isn't one of your stories. Let's bring it back to reality."

"Right," I said. "Reality." But sometimes reality was so boring. Fiction—*my* fiction—was way better. I'm pretty sure I'm the best writer in my school, where I'm a soon-to-be eighth grader.

Gianna asked, "You're totally gonna teach it to me, right?"

"It depends on if I have to take some kind of oath that could only be broken in the event of a zombie apocalypse," I said.

Dad suggested, "And let's try to cool it with apocalypse-related exaggerations, huh? Aunt Maria probably doesn't 'get' zombies and their ilk."

"Roger that, Dad," I said.

"I'm going to pack," Gianna said. "I can bring a glue gun, right? That's okay on the plane, isn't it?"

"I'm pretty sure they have glue guns in Italy. Or maybe you could refrain from hot-gluing things for two weeks," Mom suggested.

"Ha! You're funny, Mom," Gianna said. "Don't lose that sense of humor while the two of us are spending fourteen days in Italy!"

Gi and I looked at each other. "ITALY!" we both yelled at the same time.

We would've screamed way louder if we'd had any idea how much this trip would change the future—mine, Gianna's, Aunt Maria's, Amore Pizzeria's, and Rome's.

2

STAMP!

The customs officer, who sat in a glass-enclosed booth, pounded his stamp onto Gianna's passport.

I slid mine through a little hole in the glass, and he did the same.

New stamps in our passports!

"Yay!" Me and Gi high-fived.

A few moments later my eyes caught a paper sign that said LUCIA AND GIANNA ROSSI.

The lady holding it wasn't Aunt Maria. She was as

different as possible from our older Italian aunt. She was young, maybe twenty-three, and was all bright colors and peculiarities. Her head was wrapped in a dark purple scarf that hung like a long tail down her back. Her sunglasses were splotched with mismatched paint, and her pants were unlike any that I'd ever seen: one leg was striped and short and snug (maybe spandex), while the other leg was flowery, long, and flowing (possibly silk).

We made our way over to her and her sign.

"Are you Lucia and Gianna?" she asked without a trace of an Italian accent. She was as American as me.

We nodded.

"Buongiorno!" She hugged us just like Aunt Maria would have: tight, and extra long. "I'm Jane Attilio, and I've come to take you to Amore Pizzeria. *Andiamo!"*

Gi and I looked at each other, unfamiliar with the word. Maybe she didn't know that we didn't speak Italian.

"Let's go!" Jane added with a big smile. With one hand she dragged my wheely suitcase. With the other she took Gianna's hand and led us out of the airport. "We're going to have an incredibly awesome two weeks."

Jane Attilio effortlessly crammed our bags into her small European automobile (a Fiat) and whizzed us— and I do mean "whizzed"!—through the streets of Rome.

While Jane's driving was fast, it was no crazier than everyone else's. I would've buckled up twice, if that was possible.

We passed ancient and crumbling buildings and statues, monuments and ruins. When traffic stopped, we were next to a big stone wall, where a very long line of people stood.

"What are they doing?" I asked.

"Behind that wall is Vatican City. Those people are in the queue to go in." Jane pointed to a half-moon of gigantic stone columns. "That plaza is Saint Peter's Square. See that big dome behind it? That's the Basilica. People travel very far to get in there."

"So cool," I said, and snapped a picture with my cell phone.

Jane navigated the roads onto a white marble bridge called the Ponte Principe Amedeo Savoia Aosta, which took us over the Tiber—a river that ran right through the middle of the city.

Finally Jane's little car halted at the end of a cobblestone alley. "Amore Pizzeria is down there," she said.

Gianna started getting her bags out of the car and setting them down on the street.

Jane said, "That's okay. Leave your bags. I'll drop them off at Aunt Maria's apartment. It's not far." She hugged us both again, real hard. "She is so excited to see you girls. You're all she's talked about since she found out you were coming." Jane got back into the car and yelled, "I hope you'll be able to cheer her up."

Why does she need cheering up?

3

~~~

Ahhh! I recognized the smells of roasting garlic and simmering tomatoes from my great-aunt Maria's signature secret sauce. I hadn't smelled it in years.

"Lucia! Gianna!" Aunt Maria called from the kitchen through a big rectangular opening in the wall. The hole was for passing hot food from the kitchen to the dining room. It had a ledge where the cook could set plates while they waited to be picked up. "The girls are here!" She shuffled out.

Aunt Maria looked older than I remembered; her

hair, which used to be black, was now peppered with gray. She grabbed hold of me—thankfully, her snug embrace hadn't changed. She switched to hug Gianna and then back to me again. Either she'd shrunk or I'd grown—probably both—but now I was taller than her.

I said, "It's good to see you, too." After three rounds of embraces, Gianna and I were both dusted with flour from her hands and apron.

She stepped back and studied us from head to toe. "Look at you." She grew teary. "You are so *bellissima*, beautiful." She lifted the tomato-sauce-speckled apron and wiped her eyes. "I am so happy you girls are here. You are like a breath of the fresh air." She took us each by the hand and led us to a table. "Look at how skinny you are. I am getting you the pizza." She frowned at our figures, then hustled behind the counter. "Sit. Sit. It will take me one minute."

I hadn't been to Amore since first grade. Even though I didn't remember the visit well, I knew the familiar scent of spices seeping out of the walls like ghosts of old friends.

Now the pizzeria looked worn, like Aunt Maria had tried to redecorate at some point but hadn't finished. Paint covered the exposed brick wall. The chairs and tables needed attention—they were chipped, stained, and a little wobbly.

A picture of my great-uncle Ferdinando hung in the center of a wall covered with framed photos that looked like they hadn't been dusted in months, maybe years. There was a ledge holding trinkets that seemed to be layered with a thin coating of Parmesan cheese.

Aunt Maria returned with two plates and three bottles of Aranciata (an Italian orange soda that I love!). Not sure why she had brought the extra bottle. "*Mangia, mangia*," she said. "Eat, girls."

Crispy crust.

Aunt Maria's signature sauce.

Steamy, melty mozzarella cheese.

Ooey, gooey, cheesy, and crispy.

It was, like, delicious with an ice-cold glass of *mmmmm*.

We had totally hit the jackpot with these temporary summer jobs.

Let me tell you about Amore's pizza, because it's different from American pizza: First, they're round, not triangle, slices. It's like everyone gets their own small individual pie made specifically for them. And the toppings are different. The ones she brought out were smothered with roasted garlic.

"It's quiet in here," Gianna commented.

"*Sì*. There are not so much customers." Aunt Maria sighed sadly. Maybe this was why she needed cheering up. "You like the pizza?"

"It's as good as I remembered," I said through a mouthful of cheese.

Aunt Maria nestled herself into a chair across from us and exhaled as she took her weight off her feet. "I have something to tell you." She looked us both in the eye. "You cannot work here."

Splat! Those words landed like a meatball plopped onto a plate of spaghetti.

"What?" Gianna and I asked together.

"Well, one of you can," she clarified. "But not both."

One of us has to go home? But we just got here!

"How come?" Gianna asked. "What's wrong? We promise we'll work hard."

"It is not that. It is the Pizzeria de Roma." Aunt Maria spat the name. "It's an old pizzeria in the piazza by the Fontana del Cuore." That's the Fountain of the Heart. "Now it has a big new flashy sign and shiny new forks," she said. "Everybody go there. They see it right there in the piazza!"

"How's their pizza?" I asked.

"You think I know?" She pinched her fingers together and flipped her wrist back and forth as she spoke. "I never go."

"Then how do you know that they have shiny forks?" I asked.

"Signorina Jane Attilio. She live upstairs." Aunt Maria pointed up. "She see them when she walk past."

Gianna and I looked at each other. "Are you going to send one of us home?" I asked.

"No. No. No. You stay. Signorina Attilio, she says one of you can help her. She is very busy."

"Oh great," I said. "Let me guess. She works at a funeral home, or a toothpick factory, or vacuuming dirt out of USB ports?"

(I didn't think there was really any such thing as a toothpick factory.)

"What is this 'ports'? No. No," Aunt Maria said. "She is a tailor."

Gianna's eyebrows shot up. "Like, she makes things? I'm great at that."

"*Sì?*" Aunt Maria asked.

"Yeah. See these jeans?" Gianna stood and showed the rhinestone embellishments on the back pocket. "I added them myself."

"*Bella!* You are good at the designs," Aunt Maria said, admiring the bling. "You will like to work with Signorina, *sì?*"

"I think I will."

"Then you are the one," Aunt Maria said to Gianna.

Phew! I would've skinny-dipped in the Fontana del Cuore before I'd have given up working at Amore.

At that moment, a boy walked in Amore's front door. Not just any kind of a boy. He was extremely cute, with a thick head of dark hair to match his thick arm muscles. He looked like he was Gianna's age. Gianna's eyes popped out of her skull at the sight of him.

"*Buongiorno,*" he said.

"Hi," we said.

"I am Lorenzo," he introduced himself in English.

"*Tu!*" Aunt Maria pointed at him. To us she said, "I know who he is. He cannot come in here!"

4

Lorenzo set a Vera Bradley bag on the counter next to the cash register and held his hands up in surrender. "I just wanted to deliver this. It was on the ground at the end of the alley." One of Gianna's bags must not have made it back into the Fiat. "The tag says it belongs to Gianna Rossi. Since your last name is Rossi, I figured I'd bring it over. You are lucky it wasn't stolen!"

"Yup, that's mine," Gianna said. She got up and took the bag from him. The luggage tag clearly stated her name and cell phone number. "*Grazie*," she said. Her eyes locked with his.

"*Bene*." Lorenzo stared at Gianna. "You are *bellissima*," he said to her. "Pretty."

Gianna flipped a few locks of hair over her shoulder. "*Grazie*," she said again, this time with a blush and a shy smile.

I rolled my eyes at her flirty maneuver.

"Are you American?" Lorenzo asked.

"*Sì.*"

"*Vai!*" Aunt Maria yelled at him. "Go!"

Lorenzo pointed to the cell phone number on the luggage tag, moved to the door, and mouthed, "I'll call."

Through the window we watched him strap on a helmet and vroom away on a bright-red Vespa scooter with an unusually loud motor.

Aunt Maria placed her hand firmly on Gianna's. "He is with the Pizzeria de Roma. He must stay away."

"But he seems so nice," Gianna said.

"And he ain't bad to look at, if you know what I mean," I added under my breath.

"Do not think that his words and beauty are true. He is very bad. They take my customers," she said. She gave us both a look that meant business. "Promise me you will not talk to him again."

"Okay," Gianna said. I watched her cross her legs under the table. "I promise." I was pretty sure she wasn't planning to keep that promise.

"*Buono*," Aunt Maria said. "Now I tell Signorina Attilio to come down." To me she said, "I am going to teach you my sauce this summer. It is true."

"Yay!"

She shuffled to the back of the shop, picked up a broom, and klonked the handle four times on the ceiling, knocking.

Knock—knock—knock—knock.

"Are you going to stay away from him?" I asked while Aunt Maria was away.

The knocks were followed by the sound of four stomps coming from the floor above.

"You saw him. Is that even humanly possible?" Gianna asked. "Besides, it's summer break. We have two weeks in Italy, one of the most romantic places in the world. And I don't have a boyfriend."

I didn't say anything to Gianna, but I'd had a strange feeling in my gut when she spoke to Lorenzo. It was a feeling I'd been having kinda a lot lately. Like bubbles spilling over the edges of a glass of Coke.

Aunt Maria returned. "Signorina is on her way down." She left again with our dirty plates and empty bottles.

I felt something brush against my leg under the table and reached down to swat it. It wasn't something swat-table.

"Meataball!" I exclaimed. "You're alive!" I bent down to lift him for a hug. Lifting Meataball was no small task. I kissed him. "I'm so happy to see you."

Gianna said, "He's gotten *bigger*."

"And heavier." I sat down with him in my arms and scratched his ears. He purred and exposed his belly, inviting me to rub it.

As a kitten, Meataball found himself trapped in a trash can behind Amore Pizzeria. Aunt Maria kept him and called him Romeo, *her* Romeo. And Romeo, a beautiful gray tabby, grew, especially in the belly zone, and was lovingly nicknamed Meataball.

I petted him and he purred. "That is one impressive hunk of cat tummy," I laughed.

Meataball yawned.

"He's so sweet," Gianna said.

While we spoiled the cat, Jane Attilio swooped in from a door in the kitchen that was visible through the opening in the wall between the kitchen and dining room. She was now wrapped in an extraordinarily long plaid pashmina. I'm no fashion expert, but it didn't go with any of the other crazy stuff she was wearing.

She joined our table and patted Meataball's belly like someone looking for good luck from a Buddha statue.

"So, which one of you is going to work with me?" Jane poked a straw into the extra Aranciata bottle and sipped.

"Me!" Gianna raised her hand. "I love that wrap and those glasses."

"Thanks. I painted them with nail polish."

"Nail polish? Great idea. I could probably Gorilla Glue some bling on those," Gianna said.

"Bling? I love bling!"

"The bling-ier, the better, I always say," Gianna declared. She had just found a new BFF.

"Let me guess," I said to Jane. "You like mushrooms on pizza."

"It's my favorite. How did you know?"

"I haff my vays," I said with squinty sort of mysterious eyes.

Gianna glared at me with a raised eyebrow. "Don't start with that."

Jane asked, "What's 'that'?"

Gianna shook her head subtly so that only I could see. She didn't want me to tell Jane about "that."

I ignored her. I said, "'That' is my unusual ability to tell things about people based on their pizza preferences.

20

People who like mushrooms are creative types, generally; it isn't an exact science."

"That's fascinating," Jane said.

"That's not all," I said.

Gianna said, "Yes, it is."

"No," I added. "There's more."

"Do tell." Jane leaned in and flipped her nail-polished glasses onto the top of her head scarf.

The sound of a plate scraping against the tile floor came from the kitchen, and Meataball struggled to jump off my lap.

"Meataball! *Mangia!*" Aunt Maria called.

He hustled, his belly swinging beneath him, to lap up whatever had just been set on the floor for him to eat.

I explained, "Once I know someone's pizza type, I can create a couple with someone else based on *their* pizza type."

Jane asked, "Like a romantic couple?"

"She's only done it once," Gianna interjected.

I clarified, "I've only *actually* done it once, like for real, but I've made lots more couples in my head. Those should count."

"And the one you did for real, it worked?" Jane asked.

"So far," I said.

"It's only been a few weeks," Gianna said.

"Six," I said.

"This is very cool," Jane said. "You're like a live, one-girl dating service."

"Except that dating services use science or formulas," Gianna said.

"But in Italy, people like tradition. I think they'd be excited about a good old-fashioned matchmaker that they can meet face-to-face right here in a pizzeria in Rome," Jane replied.

"And," I added, "if dating services ever suddenly just disappear, due to something like a zombie apocalypse, we'll have an experienced matchmaker ready to go."

"Zombies?" Jane's face scrunched.

I remembered what Dad had said about cooling it with my stories. "Or something like zombies," I said.

5

Gianna went upstairs with Jane, while I went to the kitchen to see Aunt Maria.

"This is AJ." Aunt Maria pointed to a boy about my age who was tearing romaine lettuce into bite-size pieces. "And this is Vito." She indicated a man pounding chicken breast with a wooden mallet. "He no speak English." She said something to him in Italian, and he waved to me.

"*Buongiorno*," he said.

I waved back with a smile.

To AJ she said, "This is Lucy. I told you about her. Please show her the things around here." Aunt Maria took off her apron and hung it carefully on a hook. "I go to the bank and be here in one hour." With her black purse over her shoulder, she left through the back door.

"Hey," AJ said to me, and held out his fist for a bump, which I gave. Nothing about AJ seemed Italian: bushy blond hair, blue eyes, light skin. "Your aunt told me a lot about you."

"You know about me, but I don't know anything about you," I said. "Doesn't seem fair. What's your story, AJ?"

"Let's see, I've been working here for about a year."

"Do a lot of Americans work at pizzerias in Italy?" I asked.

"Hardly any," he said. "My dad was transferred here for his job. I started coming in here every day to pick up dinner. Sometimes I would help Maria talk to tourists or translate things for her."

"You speak Italian?"

"Not like, fluent, but I took a class in school and I had a special tutor for a few months before we moved here." He continued, "Anyway, I asked her if I could have a job. I needed the money and she needed a translator and I had some experience as a busboy. The waiter quit, so now I'm a one-man show. Let me show you around." He pointed to glass containers. "These hold oil."

"Got it. Oil."

He walked past the ovens. "This is where we cook the pizza."

"Why are they empty?"

He pointed to the dining room. "No customers." I looked at my watch. It was still set to Pennsylvania time, where it was nine in the morning. "What time is it?"

He pulled his phone out of his back pocket and checked. "Three."

"So you'll probably start getting ready for the dinner crowd soon," I said.

AJ laughed. "We can roll out some dough, but since Pizzeria de Roma reopened, we don't get crowds the way we used to. In fact, if something major doesn't happen soon, your aunt will probably close this place."

"Close it? It's been in the family for years," I said. I pointed to a faded black-and-white picture that hung on a wall in the dining room. The glass covering the picture was smudged with grease. "Do you know what this is a picture of?"

He shrugged.

"These are my great-grandparents and their six children." I pointed. "This is Aunt Maria, and this little boy is my grandfather, Luciano—I'm named after him. He left for America with his brother when he was only eight."

AJ looked unimpressed, so I added, "It took ten stormy nights by sea for them to arrive in America. They'd lost their shoes and had to walk miles through snow to meet people they were going to live with. They lost a few toes but managed to start a family." *Man, I could make up a good story.*

He'd perked up around "stormy night." I showed him another picture. "And this small house was the original Amore Pizzeria. My great-grandparents started making pizza and invited friends over on Sunday nights. The crowd grew, so they added tables into their living room. People started placing orders to bring the pizza to their own homes. Soon they had so many customers that they built a restaurant at the end of a narrow cobblestone street near Fontana del Cuore. It's been a landmark ever since."

At the last sec, I added, "It's rumored that the Pope himself orders his pizza from here under a different name."

AJ raised his eyebrows at me and said, "I think maybe you made that part up."

Sometimes a story needs extra spice. My teachers all say I'm good at those little details that make a story really interesting. Although I might go overboard sometimes.

"You may not be able to relate to this the way I can, but trust me, Amore Pizzeria can't close. I'll do whatever it takes to keep it open," I promised.

"How are you going to do that?" AJ asked.

I paused. "I don't know yet, but I will!"

He lifted his hands in an *I give up* gesture. "I believe you. I'll even help."

"Really? Why?"

"I might not be related to Maria, but I like her and I like this job. I need to save money."

"Well, let's get started with a little old-fashioned detective work," I said.

He scratched his head, signaling that he didn't understand what I meant.

"We need to spy—check out Pizzeria de Roma," I explained. "To understand what we're dealing with."

"I'm in, but don't tell Maria. She wouldn't like us going to that place."

"Roger that." I walked to the door. "*Andiamo.*" I'd figured out that meant "Let's go."

6

We strolled down the alley, which was complete with a trio of stray cats who, all put together, were smaller than Meataball. The stores—a bakery, a handbag store, and a butcher shop—that lined the quiet street were dark, closed, out of business. Sprigs of ivy that had sprung up between the cobblestones crept up the buildings' facades, and terra-cotta pots were overgrown with weeds.

"What happened to the stores?" I asked.

"The same thing that's happening at Amore," AJ said. "At the end of this road is a piazza built around the

Fontana del Cuore. There are bigger, brighter, and more modern stores there," he explained. "They may not be better, but you know what they say . . . location, location, location."

We came to the end of the alley.

I had to shade my eyes from the sun, which drenched the crowd of people in the square. It bustled with tourists snapping pictures of the ancient Roman architecture, throwing coins into the Fontana del Cuore, kissing under marble statues, and painting at easels. I had to admit that both the beauty and excitement attracted me.

There was one wide main street that led people, bikes, and motor scooters to and from the piazza. The little roads and alleyways off the square were like unnecessary tentacles around the big attraction that had everything: shops, cafés, restaurants, and carts selling souvenirs, trinkets, key chains, and Pinocchio puppets. It was strange that the crowds and hubbub were so close to Amore Pizzeria without any of it being seen. Of course, that also meant that all these people couldn't see Amore either. That was a problem.

"Isn't there a story about this fountain? I think Uncle Ferdinando told it to me once, but I can't remember it."

"You throw a coin in and wish for your true love, blah blah blah."

"Blah blah blah? You're such a guy." I looked into

the fountain. There were enough coins to make some-one very rich. Apparently, lots of people were looking for their true love.

Shining on the other side of the Fontana, like the big deal of the piazza, were multicolored letters spell-ing PIZZERIA DE ROMA. We entered. Inside, a small group of people waited near a podium for the hostess to seat them.

"I'm going to the restroom," I said, and followed an arrow down a hall. There were three doors. Two were restrooms. The third was cracked open, so I peeked in. It was a small office. There was a red motorcycle-type helmet on a desk and a pile of clothes—jeans, oxford shirt—on the floor. I wanted to go in and snoop around at the papers and files on the desk, but I was too ner-vous.

When I returned to AJ, he had moved up a bit in the line. It seemed like the hostess was super slow. The place wasn't even that busy!

"Where are you from?" I asked AJ.

"I was born in California."

"And what are you saving money for?" I asked.

"A new guitar," he said. "Right now I play the ukulele."

I asked, "Can you sing?"

"Sure. Who can't sing?"

"Well, everyone thinks they can sing, but not many actually can. Let me hear," I said.

"Now? Here?" He pointed out that we were in a crowded line.

"No time like the present," I said.

"Unless we were in the past or the future," he suggested.

I thought. "Maybe. But we're not. So, stop stalling, SpongeBob SongPants."

AJ cleared his throat. "All right." He sang, "Pizza! Ohhhh, how I love pizza!! Pizza, ba-a-a-by."

Maybe I should tell you about AJ's singing: It wasn't great, but it didn't matter, because he was cute in a California surfer kinda way. The cute and not-great (okay, "bad") singing combo somehow worked for him.

I started clapping, and everyone else joined in. A few people hooted and whooped. The crowd parted, creating a path for us to move to the front of the line. We got seated right away. I guess they must've been hungry for live music if they thought *that* was good.

Pizzeria de Roma was definitely decorated to stand out. The lights were bright, and the walls were painted lime green. It looked more like an American frozen yogurt place than a pizzeria in Rome. There was a stage and a dance floor, both covered with old-fashioned pinball machines that were unused and seemed out of place.

I studied the menu, which was not only in Italian but also in English, Spanish, French, and German. We ordered two Aranciatas and three kinds of pizza. I chose eggplant and sun-dried tomatoes. AJ went with two orders of anchovy. *Blech!*

Not surprisingly, they didn't have ham and pineapple (my fave)—that was more of an American thing.

"What do you think of this place?" AJ asked.

"It's nice, I guess. Exciting and colorful, but it lacks . . . something. . . ."

"What?" he asked.

"Tradition," I said. "I don't even feel like I'm in Italy. I don't even feel like I'm in a pizza place. I mean, this could be an arcade in Pennsylvania."

He looked around. "Yup. You're exactly right." He sipped his soda. "So, Lucy, what do you do for fun in Amer—" He snapped the menu open in front of his face.

"What are you doing?"

He stretched his mouth around the menu to talk, but kept the rest of his face hidden. "Lorenzo," he whispered.

I glanced around and caught a glimpse of him. He wore a crisply ironed white shirt with the Pizzeria de Roma logo and his name on the lapel and matching white pants under a black apron that was tied at the waist.

"Don't look!" AJ snapped.

I casually brushed my hair in front of my face and refocused my eyes to my fork. Aunt Maria was right, they were shiny.

We waited a minute.

I scanned the floor to see if Lorenzo's feet were still there. "He's gone."

AJ lowered his menu. "That was close."

Just then, a waitress appeared with our pizzas. I had to admit, they looked really good.

I hung my nose into the steam. "Smells good," I said. I cut a piece of eggplant, closed my eyes, and slid it into my mouth. I let it sit on my tongue for a second. Then I opened my eyes.

"What?" AJ asked.

I didn't answer, just chewed and swallowed.

"Good?" he asked. "Do you like it?"

Again, I didn't answer. I cut a piece with sun-dried tomatoes. Again, I put it in my mouth, closed my eyes, and let my tongue roll around it.

When I opened my eyes this time, I saw that AJ had finished both of his anchovy pies. BOTH!

How do boys do that?

Through a full mouth, he asked, "Good?"

"No. The crust is doughy and undercooked. And

Aunt Maria's sauce blows this away. This could be"—I lowered my voice—"from a jar."

I looked at all the people in the crowded restaurant. "Look, there's no, 'Ooh. Mmmm.' Or 'This is so good.' They're only here because it's convenient. There's nothing special or memorable about this place except maybe the big dance floor, but they don't even use that. The food is like blah with a side of meh." I smiled and pushed the food away. "This is great!" I said.

"You just said it was 'meh.'"

"That's what's great. Amore Pizzeria is way better. We just need something to attract customers. And the place could use a little sprucing up, if you know that I mean. Luckily, I know the Queen of Bling, who can help with a makeover."

"I like your optimism." AJ eyed my plate. "You going to eat that?" I slid the plate to him. "Do you have a good idea for how to attract customers?" he asked.

I grinned. "Actually, I have *two* good ideas."

7

My ideas: samples and couples.

The next day I started with samples. I rolled the dough for a big pizza, very thin like my dad had taught me—of course he learned from Aunt Maria. I planned to top it with cheese, Aunt Maria's sauce, and an amazing classic Italian topping, sausage. Its deliciousness would lure people down the narrow cobblestone alley. Once they arrived, I'd match them. Then word would spread—maybe it would even trend on social media. All those coin throwers looking for love would come here. If my plan worked, I'd spend the rest of my visit teaching Aunt Maria how to match when I was gone.

Hmmm . . . I should probably start keeping good notes to share with her.

In the kitchen with me was Vito, the cook who didn't speak English. He packed a meat mixture into balls and hummed loudly.

Then I heard something else, a sound coming from a vent near one of the ovens.

It was Gianna's voice from Jane Attilio's apartment upstairs.

I listened harder, but AJ came into the kitchen and interrupted my eavesdropping.

He had tied a red bandanna around his head in a rock star kind of way.

"I want one," I said about the bandanna. He pulled one out of a drawer. My hands were floury, so he tied it for me in a Little Red Riding Hood style—under my chin.

He laughed.

Even I chuckled a little before saying, "Come on, like yours."

He switched it to the back of my head over my long, curly hair. I took a quick peek at my reflection in the stainless-steel oven door; it actually looked cool.

Just then Meataball rubbed against my legs. "Is there another bandanna?" I asked AJ.

He handed one to me, and I tied it around Meataball's neck, so he could be included. He purred.

"So, what are we doing here?" AJ asked.

"Making samples, just like the food court at the mall. It works there. Maybe it will here." I brushed on more sauce, making sure to get all the way to the edges. I dipped a spoon into the sauce and put just a smidgen on my lips. "I just love it. I swear I could sit in this pot all day, like a sauce hot tub."

"I'd go in with you," he said. "We'd need a big pot." He rolled out his own crust and swirled sauce on it.

"What's your fave topping?" I asked.

"Duh! Anchovies."

"Really?" This was a drag. In my experience, ham and pineapple wasn't a match with anchovies. At least I didn't think so. After all, I was still a beginner at this matching stuff.

I finished off my pizza with fresh mozzarella and Italian sausage, with a dash of Parmesan cheese and oregano.

AJ put my masterpiece on a wooden board and showed me how to slide the pizza into the oven and take the board out.

"Do you have little plates that we can serve the samples on?" I asked.

"White paper pie plates?" He indicated a stack resembling the Leaning Tower of Pisa, which I'd called the Leaning Tower of Pizza until, like, two years ago.

If Gianna was here, she'd have used fancy scrapbook scissors to give each plate pretty edges and then decorated them with markers and glitter, and maybe hung ribbon from the bottom. "They'll work."

AJ looked into the pizza oven. "It's done." He went to open it, but I put my hand on the silver handle keeping it closed.

"A few more seconds for *extra* crispiness."

"One Mississippi, two Mississippi, three Mississippi, four—get the pizza cutter—Mississippi," he said.

I grabbed the rolling pizza cutter.

"Five—I think this is a good idea—Mississippi," he said. "Six—and it smells good—Mississippi."

I said, "Seven—but you also liked Pizzeria de Roma's yucky pizza—Mississippi."

He said, "Eight—I was really hungry—Mississippi."

"Nine—you're going to love this—Mississippi."

"Ten—can we stop now—Mississippi?"

"Yes—Mississippi."

AJ opened the oven door and in one quick swoop

slid the wooden board under my rectangular pizza, gently removed it, and carried it to a cutting board that was lightly sprinkled with flour. AJ smacked the round cutter into the crust and quickly ran it from one side to the other, making bite-size squares. I put each one on a paper plate.

Soon I'd filled a tray. "Are you going to try one?" I asked.

"Duh."

We each took a square. I crunched into mine and enjoyed the melted cheese and salty Italian sausage.

AJ said, "Mmm. *So* good."

"That's the reaction we're looking for. Let's go before it gets cold."

On our way out, a deliveryman who reminded me of a tanned Santa Claus came in the back door with bread. "*Buongiorno!*" he cried with a huge smile.

"*Buongiorno!*" I returned the same excitement and gave him a sample.

"*Delizioso!*" His stomach shook like a bowl full of jelly.

We left the cook and deliveryman speaking in rapid-fire Italian and strolled down the alley. I looked in each of the closed shops and thought about how sad it was that these businesses had closed because more modern stores had opened on the main piazza. That was sad with a scoop of bummer on top.

We stood at the end of the piazza opposite Pizzeria de Roma, in sight of the crowds of people—both tourists and locals.

I called, "Amore Pizzeria here! Free samples!"

People looked but didn't come over. I tried again, "Come and get your free sample from Amore Pizzeria!"

A couple of tourists—fanny packs are a dead giveaway—came over.

"Help yourself." I held out the tray.

I saw a girl looking at me from a distance. I called to her, "Would you like to try a free sample? Bring your friends, too."

Soon I was surrounded by people. When *other* people saw the crowd, they came over to see what was going on too. I called out, "This pizza is from Amore, which is behind me at the end of that cute street. It's traditional pizza made with a signature secret sauce that's been passed down for generations. My aunt Maria won't even tell me what's in it. That's how secret it is!"

(Like I said, a good story has a select few perfect details. Like telling them the sauce was from a secret family recipe. People love that stuff!)

Everyone smiled and seemed to enjoy their pizza

samples. Several started walking down the quiet little alley.

I said, "Maybe you should get crust ready at the shop."

"Roger that," AJ said, copying my trademark phrase I'd used earlier. He grinned at me, showing off his dimples.

I can't believe someone this cute could like anchovies.

8

I entertained the sample-eating crowd. "Aunt Maria goes to the vegetable auction every three days for the best, naturally ripe tomatoes." I added, "To keep the recipe secret, she does it late at night when no one's around. She learned from her mother, who learned from her mother. It's written down and locked in a safe that can only be opened upon her death. Her last will and testament specifies which family member will inherit the recipe."

I didn't know that any of this was true, but I didn't know for a fact that it was *untrue*.

The crowd oohed and aahed about the samples and listened to every word.

I said, "Amore Pizzeria is just at the end of this street. Come on down for some traditional Italian pizza. I can smell it from here!"

My tray was empty, and a small group of people started moving toward the alley.

With part one of my two-part plan complete, I hustled back to the restaurant, where three tables had seated themselves and more customers waited by the door.

AJ took orders and delivered drinks. When he walked past me, he said, "More samples are finished in the oven."

"Roger that," I said. I quickly swished the board under the rectangular pie and cut it the way AJ had shown me. Then I walked around the shop, making personal deliveries and refilling drinks—mostly Cokes and fizzy water that they called *acqua frizzante*. I pointed to the family pictures on the walls and explained who was who. There were some people I didn't know much about, so I made up stories about them to keep customers amused until their lunches arrived.

"Grab those dishes and follow me." AJ indicated steaming bowls of spaghetti—of course Amore served more than pizza—that Vito had set on the counter between the kitchen and dining room.

Aunt Maria walked in the front door, followed by a man in a business suit.

"My goodness," she said. "Busy lunch today."

"Yes," I said.

She introduced the man, "This is Eduardo Macelli from the bank."

I smiled. "Hi. Welcome to Amore Pizzeria. Will you be having lunch?"

"*Sì*," he said.

"Follow me to this table just beneath a beautiful painting of the very port that my grandfather sailed from on his way to America. His name was Luciano. I was named after him," I said. "My name is Lucy."

Eduardo Macelli sat down. He was a petite man, bald and thin.

"Let me guess," I said, studying him. "*Acqua fizzante*?"

"*Sì*."

I returned to the kitchen, where Aunt Maria checked her sauce supply. "Be sure he gets the best service," she said to me about Eduardo Macelli.

"I will." I took him the last sample with his fizzy water. He bit into it. I waited for a reaction but didn't get one.

"Do you like it?"

"*Sì*." It seemed Eduardo Macelli wasn't much of a talker.

I asked, "Do you know what kind of pizza you want?"

"Surprise me," he said with a thick Italian accent and a straight face.

"I'll do that."

I wrote down one ricotta cheese and one salami. Those might be unusual in America but were pretty standard here in Rome. I gave the order slip to AJ, because I wasn't sure where it was supposed to go next.

Then I watched the customers and started making couples in my head. Since the pizza toppings here were so different from the ones at home, I sort of had to start from scratch. I had pepperoni, mushrooms, and meatball all worked out, but ricotta cheese and salami were new territory for me. This required serious concentration.

A pretty woman with a cute pink purse was speaking French with her female companion while savoring *bianca* (that's white pizza) with asparagus and burrata mozzarella—a cheese with a smooth, creamy center that's spreadable. It is majorly *delizioso*.

A table of four men nearby had ordered a table-size margarita pizza. (Margarita is topped with olive oil, garlic, fresh basil, tomatoes, and mozzarella and Parmesan cheeses.)

When I passed them, my stomach fluttered like a

butterfly had just burst out of a cocoon. And an idea hit me.

AJ had added up checks for the tables. "I'll deliver those," I offered.

First I gave Eduardo Macelli his pizza. Then I placed a leather folio containing a check on the table with the French ladies and gave another to the men eating margarita.

Then I watched and waited.

When the ladies realized I'd given them the wrong bill, they scanned the tables for the order matching the food on the check.

Mademoiselle bianca with asparagus and burrata mozzarella approached one of the margarita men. "*Pardonnez-moi*," she said in French. Then in English she said, "I think this is your check."

Mr. Margarita opened the folio. "And this is the one for you," he said with an Italian accent.

They traded, pausing for only a second when they each had a hand on the same folio.

The butterflies in my stomach flapped their wings.

"What is your name?" he asked.

"Murielle."

He said, "Would you and your friend join us for coffee, Murielle?"

"*Bien sûr*. Of course."

The ladies fitted chairs around the men's table, and AJ brought them espresso and cappuccino.

My first match!

I found a pad used for taking orders and jotted notes about matching margarita and bianca pizzas.

AJ leaned on the counter. "What happened there?"

"Remember I told you that I had two ideas? The samples were just to get people here. That"—I pointed to the table—"is my second idea. You see, I'm kind of a . . . a bit of a . . . I guess you'd call it a . . . romance coordinator. I—"

"Lucy." Aunt Maria waved for me to come into the kitchen.

"I'll tell you later," I said to AJ, and headed to Aunt Maria.

AJ called after me, "Uh, yeah. You will. You can't just tell someone that and walk away."

I turned. "Sorry." Once in the kitchen, I asked Aunt Maria, "What's up?"

"What was that with the check?"

"I thought I would introduce *them*"—I indicated the women—"to *them*." I indicated the men.

"Why?"

"Well, because of the pizza they ordered," I con-fessed. "You see, I kind of guess things about people based on how they like their pizza. Something told me that the margarita and bianca people would make a good romantic match."

"*Mamma mia!*" Aunt Maria exclaimed. "Who taught you to do that?"

"No one. It was just like a feeling I had in my gut one day at home at a pizza shop. And I went with it. First it was just in my head. Then I tried it for real. And it worked!"

"It is the *matchmaking*. It is not good. Do not mess with the love."

"But it could be good for business," I said. "Look around. They'll totally Instagram and tweet this stuff."

"What is this 'tweet'? Like a bird?" She shook her head, not really wanting an explanation. "No. No more, Lucy. Understand? *Capisce?*"

I sighed. "All right. But it seems a shame to let this skill go to waste."

"No more! Don't mess with the love."

"Okay," I said. I walked back out to the dining room, angry and confused. Why did it bother her so much?

I walked right past AJ without explaining anything and approached Mr. Macelli. "Did you like the pizza?" I asked him.

"Yes. *Buono.* Now I'll try"—he pointed to two items on the menu—"this and this."

"You're still hungry? Super!" I said. "I'll get that for you." I took his glass. "And I'll refill this."

I put the order in, brought the drink, and waited on other tables. As the lunch crowd faded, I wiped down tables and reset them for dinner.

Eduardo Macelli sat for another hour, determined to try as many menu items as he could before exploding. He had taken a pen and paper out of his briefcase and wrote things down.

"Can I get you anything else?" I finally asked him.

"Sì. Your *zia* Maria."

"Okay." I thought he was going to file a complaint about my waitressing or the food. "Is everything okay? This is my first day."

"Everything is *buono*. I want to talk."

I pulled Aunt Maria away from the food prep area, where she was peeling garlic, and sent her to Eduardo's table. She wrung her hands nervously as she approached him.

I walked past the table several times, lingering to catch what they were saying, but I couldn't translate their hushed Italian tones.

What was going on with those two?

9

After all the customers had left, I was so tired that I would've been happy with a cereal bar and a bed. But then I saw the spread of Italian food that Aunt Maria had set on a table in the dining room, and I forgot all about a cereal bar.

A mountain of homemade pasta with an Aunt Maria–invented sauce that had a pinkish tint to it, a chopped salad with vegetables of every color, and crusty bread wooed me to sit at the table set for seven.

"What's all this?" I asked.

"We will eat together," Aunt Maria said. She poured olive oil on little plates and sprinkled it with seasoning. "Sit." She broke off a piece of bread and dipped it in the oil. No one butters bread in Italy.

As if on cue, Gianna, Jane, and a young guy my age, looking absurd in a mid-length black skirt with many layers of pink tulle underneath, entered Amore Pizzeria through the back door.

"Ah, Rico. Here is Lucy. You remember her, sì?" She dashed into the kitchen, calling for AJ and Vito.

"Remember what?" I asked him, confused.

He shrugged. "I guess she meant that she told me you were coming. It's all she's talked about for days," he said. He popped a chunk of bread in his mouth.

"You don't have an Italian accent either," I said to Rico.

"Nope. I was born in the US. But my parents are Italian. We moved back when I was, like, six," he explained. "A lot of tourists come into Amore Pizzeria. It helps Maria to have fluent English speakers around."

That all made sense to me.

AJ sat down and asked Rico, "You the model again?"

Rico said, "Seems that I have the best legs." He jutted his bruised and battered typical boy leg out for everyone to see.

As far as banged-up boy legs go, I guessed his were pretty good. But it wasn't his legs that struck me; it was something about his eyes—dark, dark brown—that was strangely familiar. He reminded me of a boy I sometimes put in my stories.

Did I know him from somewhere? Were we online friends?

I didn't think so. A cute Italian boy who didn't mind wearing a skirt seemed like something I would remember. I got a weird feeling in my gut. Was it telling me to match him with someone? I didn't even know what kind of pizza he liked.

Rico said to me, "I know this might look weird to you, but I'm an unusual guy. I like football, snakes, loud music, horror movies, and"—he indicated the skirt—"I happen to have a knack for fashion. And, FYI, I don't usually wear skirts."

"You're right. That *is* unusual. But I like that." I whispered, "I'm a little different myself."

"Yeah? How?" he asked.

"Maybe I'll tell you one of these days."

"I can't wait."

Gianna looked at me talking to Rico and raised an eyebrow. Recently she'd been asking me if I thought there were any cute boys at school, if I liked anyone, etc.

Maybe she thought it was somehow her responsibility as my older sister to show me how to meet boys. She dropped her brow and said, "Dinner looks great. I'm so hungry."

Rico said, "Those are Maria's favorite three words to hear." His name and appearance were blatantly Italian— dark hair, skin, and eyes—but he had no accent. It seemed that Aunt Maria had somehow attracted Americans.

Aunt Maria said to everyone, "*Mangia.*" Then she called, "Meataball! Psst! Psst!"

The cat ran in and sat on his haunches next to a plate of fettuccini that Aunt Maria had cut up and put on the floor for him.

"It's his favorite," AJ said to me.

Then she dished out a generous bowl of pasta for each of us. My stomach growled at the squishy sound of the white cream sauce hitting the plate. I hadn't realized how hungry I was.

"Did you work hard today?" Aunt Maria asked Gianna.

Gianna said, "Jane and Rico don't stop. Not even for lunch."

Aunt Maria said, "Then you eat a big dinner, like AJ."

AJ twirled pasta around his fork, making sure no noodle went astray. Then he crammed the forkful into his mouth. "You can always count on me to be hungry," he said through the mouthful of pasta.

We didn't talk for a few minutes while we all took the edge off our hunger. Then I asked, "What happened with Eduardo Macelli today?"

Gianna asked, "Who's that?"

Aunt Maria said, "He is a man from the bank."

"Did he agree to give you an extension?" Jane asked.

"We are a . . . a bit behind in some of our payments since Pizzeria de Roma reopened," Aunt Maria explained. "But Eduardo Macelli is going to give me an extra month. This is good."

"That's great news," Jane said. She held up her Coke. "*Salute!*" she said.

We all repeated, "*Salute!*"

"What changed his mind?" Jane asked.

"He loved the food and thought there was a lot of customers," Aunt Maria said. Then she asked, "What happened? Why so many customers today?"

I explained about the samples and the stories on the square. "It seems they like good food, a good story, and a traditional Italian experience. You can give them that," I said.

You can give them more, but you put the kibosh on matchmaking.

"You know," I said, looking around the restaurant. "The place could use a little refresh."

"Refresh?" Aunt Maria asked.

Gianna clapped her hands. "Oh, I'm so good at refreshing. We can go with colors like red wine and espresso brown. And we can get fresh plants and cut flowers and pretty little candles on the tables. Plus, it will give me something to do while I'm here, since I'm not working in the shop."

Aunt Maria looked around. "Maybe the place does need a—what you call it?—refresh."

Gianna said, "It's kind of a big job. We're gonna need some help."

"No worries." Rico leaned back in his chair. "I know a few guys who can come over." He crossed his bruised legs under the pink pouffy skirt.

"I'll help too," I volunteered.

AJ's mouth was full again, so he raised his hand, indicating he would help too.

Gianna walked around, explaining her vision for Amore Pizzeria's face-lift. "A mirror could go here, and I can dress up all these frames and rehang them."

"I have any dress-up supply you could ever need," Jane offered.

"And I never travel without my bling kit," Gianna

said. "Then we can get a few trees, maybe a ficus, and wrap them in little white lights—a very classy and romantic feel."

Romance. That was exactly the direction I wanted to go. But *noooooooo*.

"I'll make a new curtain," Jane added.

"Oh, and get this: when it gets dark, we can line both sides of the street with LUMINARIES!" Gianna squealed. "Oh, I love, love, *love* luminaries."

Aunt Maria said, "This sounds all very good, but like a lot of money."

Rico said, "I know a guy who owns a florist shop. He owes me a favor. He can bring the stuff you need."

"Okay. Is a good idea. A little refresh," Aunt Maria relented. "Tomorrow is Wednesday and we no open. This is the day I go around Rome for my ingredients and make sauce. Can you do it in one day?"

"Totes," Gianna promised. "Except for the walls. It could take some time to get that paint off the brick. We can do that at night. The rest is easy peasy."

"'Totes'?" Aunt Maria looked confused. "'Peasy'?"

10

The next morning I found Gianna in the pizzeria early. She studied the current decor with a tilted head and occasionally wrote things on a clipboard. She would DIY this place from falling apart to fabulous.

"Aloha!" Rico said, walking through the back door. No skirt today. Ripped jeans and worn black basketball high-tops.

Aloha? Random.

Rico led three people who I guess were his "guys." Their tool belts told me they were ready to work. He said, "These are my friends." I gave them a wave. "They're good at hammering and stuff."

"I'm sure Gi has stuff to hammer," I said. "I'll head upstairs to see if I can help Jane with curtains, but I'm not really the sewing type."

"Okay, but promise me one thing." He looked very serious.

"What?"

"Please help her choose the colors. She is an amazing designer, but her fabric selecting? Ugh!" He covered his face.

"I'll do my best," I said, but the truth was that I was kind of "ugh" myself.

Jane dashed from one side of the apartment to the other, throwing around balls of yarn, yards of fabrics, spools of thread, and measuring tape. I had to duck or a flying sketch pad would've clocked me right in the noggin.

"Redecorating Amore Pizzeria is a great idea, Lucy," Jane said excitedly without looking up from her searching.

If she thought that was good, she hadn't heard my best idea of all. "Thanks."

"Here it is." She pulled a key ring with swatches of fabric from under a stack of fashion magazines and flipped through them. "Oh, I can't decide. I like this one and this one and this one. And this one is pretty." She stared at them. "Hmmm . . . What do you think?"

"Um, I'm really not great at this stuff." I remembered what Rico had said. "Maybe we should call for backup."

She nodded and stomped on the floor four times.

Bam—bam—bam—bam.

"We'll ask Rico," she said. "He has a great eye for color."

"I wouldn't have guessed," I said.

"Why?"

"Maybe because he's a boy."

"True, but he's a boy with an eye for fashion," she said. "A good eye too. I like that he is confident enough to be this tough guy who likes typical boy stuff, but this stuff too."

I nodded. That *was* pretty cool.

I was walking around the apartment/sewing studio waiting for Rico, when I heard a sound coming from downstairs. I walked toward it. It floated up from a vent. The same way I had heard what was happening up here when I was in the kitchen, I could hear people downstairs.

It was Gianna. She said, "What are you doing here? My aunt would flip out if she knew."

The only person I could imagine she would say that to was Lorenzo from Pizzeria de Roma. He was here early.

I didn't like that Lorenzo was in Amore's kitchen. I had just made up that stuff about the recipe being locked in a safe. For all I knew, it was written on a Post-it or sitting on a counter somewhere.

I heard Lorenzo say, "I wanted to tell you something."

I waved to Jane. "Come here. Listen," I whispered.

She bent toward the vent.

"Really, you can't be in the shop," Gianna said. "Maybe we can go out for a walk or something?"

Lorenzo asked, "Can I have a Coke?"

Rico walked into the apartment to find Jane and me crouched on the floor. "Looks like fun," he said.

We both shushed him.

"Jeez," he said, and bent down next to us.

Lorenzo was saying, "I am very thirsty."

Gianna said, "Fine. I'll get you some Coke, but then you have to leave."

"*Sì*. That is good."

I could hear Gianna's wooden sandals clopping on the floor as she left the kitchen and walked to the bar area, where the soda was kept in a refrigerator. I wished I could see what Lorenzo was doing.

Gianna and her shoes came back in. "Here you go."

"*Grazie*," he said. Then he exclaimed, "Whoa! That is a *grande* cat."

"Lots of him to love," Gianna said, and I imagined her scratching Meataball's ears.

Then I guess Lorenzo had sipped his soda, because he said, "Oh! It is great. And you know what else is great? You. You look very pretty today. I love your hair."

"Thank you," Gianna said. She was probably twirling a lock of it and blushing.

Rico whispered, "He's smooth."

"Shhh!" we snapped at him.

"What was that?" we heard Lorenzo ask downstairs. Had he heard us?

"Some friends who are helping me redecorate," Gianna said.

"What are you redecorating?" Lorenzo asked.

"The dining room," Gianna said. "Did you have something to tell me?"

"Sì, I came to tell you that I would like to see you again," Lorenzo said. "I want to show you Rome. Can I come get you later?"

"I'd like to see you, too," Gianna said. "Maybe I can sneak out for a while. Text me."

We heard the back door of the restaurant close.

Rico laughed, "She's a rebel, defying your aunt Maria. Not many people do that."

But if she had, maybe I could too. . . .

"Love makes people do crazy things," Jane pointed out.

"They just met," Rico argued. "How could it be love?"

"You don't believe in love at first sight?" I asked.

"I think maybe there is a spark or something at first sight," he said. "But—"

"Shh," I said, because I heard another sound. Noises came from downstairs: boxes sliding on the floor, the walk-in refrigerator opening and closing, and the whistling of a cheerful tune.

"It's just the deliveryman," Rico said. "He's here, like, every day."

Rico took his messenger-style bag, which hung diagonally across his chest, and tossed it into a chair. "You banged on the floor. What did you need?"

Jane held up the four swatches.

"Curtains?" he asked.

Jane nodded.

"This one." He chose the plainest of the three. "It'll be perfect."

"Wow," I said. "That was fast."

He shrugged. "I have an eye. Not sure if it's a blessing or a curse."

"You mean because fashion and sewing are usually for girls?"

"No. That doesn't bother me. I meant because

everyone always wants my fashion advice. I get lots of calls and texts from guys who want me to help them pick out clothes for a job interview or a date."

"Do you help them?" I asked.

"Yeah. I have a gift, and it wouldn't be fair if I didn't use it to help people who need me," he said. "But I get something too. Then I can call and ask them for favors. It's not a bad deal."

"I guess that explains all the guys you know."

"Yep."

He picked up the worn leather bag, tossed it over his shoulder, and said, "And for the record, fashion isn't just for girls."

"Oh. Sorry. You're right."

"Don't sweat it." His cell phone rang. He answered it, and after a few one-word responses, he said, "I gotta go for a while, but I'll be back."

"A fashion emergency?"

"My mom. I left without cleaning my room," he said. "She gets mad about stuff like that." He shrugged.

"Mine gets mad about that too," I said.

As he left, I got another weird feeling, like I'd seen him do that shrug before. But I couldn't have seen him do that before—I'd just met him yesterday.

Weird.

11

It was late in the day and time to show Aunt Maria what we'd done with the dining room.

She'd finished making sauce a few hours earlier and had gone to her apartment for a nap. AJ, Rico, Gianna, and I were sweeping the tile floor when Jane pushed the door open with her butt.

One of Jane's hands covered Aunt Maria's eyes while the other guided her to sit on a stool. Jane held the door open with her foot for an extra second, allowing Meataball to waddle in behind them.

"I found her baking at the apartment," Jane said. A basket of something steamy hung from her wrist.

"Thank goodness," AJ said. "I'm starving."

"I cannot wait to see what you kids have done." Aunt Maria giggled.

Gianna said, "One, two, three, TA-DA!"

Jane moved her hand.

"*Mamma mia!*" Aunt Maria cried. "It look so lovely. How did you do all of this so fast?" She wiped away a tear.

"Rico's friends were very helpful," Gianna explained. She started the tour with the biggest wall. "The pictures are in their same frames, but I added an antique finish, so they all match." They'd been hung in a lovely pattern around a huge mirror whose frame was also antiqued. The mirror made the whole dining room look bigger and brighter.

Gianna continued, "Each table has fresh-cut flowers. The tablecloths, which Rico hemmed, match the curtains." To Rico and Jane she said, "Thank you."

"What can I say?" Rico sipped espresso from a little white mug. He had proven that he was as good with a hammer as he was with a sewing machine—definitely an interesting combination for a teenage boy.

"The seats have been re-covered with black fabric."

Gianna held one up to show everyone. "Tonight while we're all sleeping, someone is coming to scrape the paint off the brick. *That* will really look great, but it might take several nights."

"*Perfetto!*" Aunt Maria gasped. "Since Ferdinando passed away, I have not been keeping up on these things."

"The menus need updating too," Gianna said. "I'll work on that tomorrow."

"Can I help?" I asked Gianna. "I have a few ideas for some new pizzas—with a little American inspiration, if you know what I mean."

"Sure," Gianna agreed. "You can help me before I show it to Aunt Maria for her approval."

Aunt Maria gave Gianna the first big hug, then the rest of us. "You must all be very tired. Why don't you get some rest?" She pulled a napkin away from the contents of her basket and a puff of sugary sweetness floated upward, covering the smell of cleaning products. "Not without a little food in your stomachs. Something that will stick to your ribs."

Let me tell you about a warm *sfogliatella* pastry. It's amazing with a side order of WOW.

"Oh yeah!" Rico grabbed a pastry and left the restaurant. I watched him through the front window as he rode away on his bike. Rico was an interesting guy. Probably pepperoni or onion. It was hard to peg. I wished I could figure out who he reminded me of. Someone—but I couldn't put my finger on it.

I was almost too tired to eat. Almost. So I took a pastry and walked out the front door, practically bumping into a woman on my way.

"Oh, *pardon*. So sorry." It was the French woman from yesterday, a.k.a. Bianca with asparagus and burrata mozzarella cheese.

Gianna said, "We're closed on Wednesdays."

"*Oui*. I know. I came to talk"—she gestured toward me—"to you."

"Huh? Me? Why?" I asked, confused.

"You mixed up my lunch check yesterday with Angelo's." She sighed when she said his name.

"Angelo?"

"The man at the other table." That must be the man who'd ordered the margarita pizza. "We walked around Rome all afternoon. We have so much in common," she said. "I just wanted to say thank you. So, *merci!*"

Gianna whispered to me, "You didn't?"

"Just a little," I whispered back. "She was the only one. Aunt Maria saw and told me, 'No mess with the love.'" I imitated Aunt Maria.

The woman heard me. "Mess with love?" she asked.

"You see, I think maybe I can make love matches based on what pizza people order," I explained. "No biggie. But I tried it on you and Angelo."

"Not *maybe*. You can!" she squealed. "You're a *matchmaker*? *C'est fantastique!*" She held out her hand. "I am Murielle duPluie. I used to be quite a popular TV news reporter in Paris. Now I work for the Rome newspaper. All of Rome needs to know about this. I will come back tomorrow with a photographer." She looked out into the open air and moved her hand along words that weren't there. "Pizzeria Matchmaker."

Gianna and I stared at the imaginary letters.

"You may get famous," Murielle duPluie said. "And Amore Pizzeria, too!" She skipped down the alley. I looked at it for a minute and imagined what it would look like lined with luminaries on either side.

"Wait," Gianna called out after her, but Murielle duPluie had already lifted her cell phone to her ear. Gianna said to me, "That's not good."

"It's not *good*; it's great! Maybe I am a"—I looked out into the open air and moved my hand along words that weren't there—"Pizzeria Matchmaker! Just think, people could get awesome food and meet the love of their life. What could be better?" Without waiting for an answer, I said, "If Amore Pizzeria is famous, it'll make lots of money and stay in business. That's the best thing we can do for Aunt Maria."

"I don't know, Lucy. You know what Aunt Maria said. I don't think she'll go for it."

"She wouldn't *if she knew*."

"You're not gonna tell her?" Gianna asked. "I think she'll notice a reporter and photographer in her restaurant."

"Not if we get her out for a few hours."

"How are we gonna do that?" Gianna asked.

"I have an idea."

Gianna grinned. "You always do."

12

The next day, well rested and refreshed, Gianna and I walked from Aunt Maria's apartment to Amore Pizzeria.

"You think it'll work?" she asked.

"Yep," I said. "When I give you the sign, you go for it. Until then, act totally normal." I handed her the slip of paper she would need to get Aunt Maria out of the pizzeria for a few hours.

"Fine, but for the record, I don't like this."

I said, "Okay. I'll make a note in the official record." I pretended to open a big, heavy book. I grunted when I opened its huge cover. I dipped an imaginary quill pen in ink and as I wrote, I said, "Gianna doesn't like it." I put the pen back in the ink cup, closed the giant book, and said, "Done."

Gianna rolled her eyes at me.

We found Aunt Maria kneading dough as AJ filled salt and pepper shakers.

I gave Gianna the signal—a thumb in my ear and wiggling my other four fingers.

Gianna flipped through some papers and said, "Oh, Aunt Maria, there's a phone message here for you."

Aunt Maria was up to her elbows in dough. "What's it say, the message?"

"Um—it's from the bank, I think. Um, I'm not sure."

Snap! Gianna was gonna crack under the pressure; I could feel it. Gianna Rossi could sneak around with Lorenzo from Pizzeria de Roma, but ask her to feed a fake phone message to Aunt Maria, and she crumbled like a block of extra-sharp Asiago cheese.

I took the slip of paper and read it. "It's from Eduardo Macelli. He wants to meet you at the bank at one o'clock. It says you should bring your business plan."

"The business plan?! That is all the way across the city with my friend Anna. She is very smart with the numbers."

"Maybe she can e-mail it to—" Gianna started saying, but I stomped on her foot. "Ah!" she cried.

Aunt Maria ignored her. "E-mail? Pfft! I take the bus. That's how we get things done. On the bus. I do not need the e-mail or the wonder web."

"You mean the World Wide Web?" Gianna asked. "The Internet?"

"Neither of these. If I want to tell you something, I call on the telephone. Not this kind"—she pointed to my cell phone with floury hands—"the regular kind. Or I write a letter with the paper and pen. Remember paper?"

"Yes. I remember paper," I said. "So, if you have to take the bus all the way to your friend's apartment before the bank, you should probably leave around noon. And I guess you won't be back until two, right? Because you'll have to bring the plan back to your friend."

She studied the wall clock. "Sì. Two. *Mamma mia!* I'll miss lunch. That is no good."

"Don't you *mamma mia* yourself. We'll be cool," I reassured her. "We can totally handle it. It's like, mega cool."

"What is this 'mega cool'?"

"She means it's all fine," Gianna said. "We can handle it. Jane, Rico, and I will help."

Aunt Maria looked at AJ.

"It's okay," he added. "I'm all over it."

"All over what? I just want you working at the lunch. Do not go all over anything," Aunt Maria said to him. She stirred sauce, checked on a tray of lasagna that was cooking in the oven, and gave a whole bunch of instructions to Vito, the cook who didn't speak English. At exactly noon, she hung her apron up and left through the back door.

"What are you gonna do when she goes to the bank and Eduardo Macelli doesn't know what she's talking about?" Gianna asked.

AJ interrupted, "Do I want to know what's going on?"

"No!" Gianna and I both said to him.

I said to Gianna, "Don't worry about Eduardo Macelli. He won't be at the bank. I took care of that."

The back door opened. It was Rico. "*Aloha*, pizzeria peeps," he said to AJ and Vito. "And Madame Big Idea."

"Big idea?" AJ asked. "Are you talking about the matchmaking?"

"I was talking about the redecorating," Rico said. "But matchmaking sounds . . . well . . . weird."

"I don't believe in matchmakers," AJ said.

Rico said, "I definitely want to hear more about this, but I understand there's a rogue chair cover needing attention pronto." He held up a staple gun as if it was a chain saw. "It had better prepare to be stapled."

"I'll get that." Gianna took the stapler from him. "We don't want anyone getting hurt."

"You can use a staple gun?" Rico asked her.

"You should see what I can do with duct tape." She ran out and pounded the silver stapler into the chair. That flapping piece of fabric didn't stand a chance.

I asked AJ, "How do the samples look?"

He said, "Almost done!"

There was a knock at the back door. Rico opened it and held it for the deliveryman with the big Santa Claus belly. Santa pushed in a wheeled cart stacked with pasta—gnocchi, linguini, ravioli, and cavatelli. "*Buongiorno!*" he cried.

Then the front door opened, and potential matches walked in. Through the opening between the kitchen and dining room, I said, "Welcome to Amore Pizzeria."

I glanced at Gianna. She sighed. "Go ahead. Do your thing."

"Now? You're doing it *now*?" AJ whispered. "The matchmaking?"

"Yep," I said. "Here it goes."

"I gotta see this," Rico said. The three of them stood at the counter between the kitchen and dining room, leaned on their elbows, and watched me work my magic.

13

"What kind of pizza do you like?" I asked the first pair of women.

"Kalamata olives," one of them said. "We get it every time, but we've never had it here."

"You'll love it." I started thinking about a match for kalamata olives. People in America usually don't get that, so I figured it would be the same as black olives, which I would probably match with mushrooms, but it wasn't an exact science. I had a hunch about what else might do the trick. And if my plan worked like I hoped it would, the match I was looking for would come through the door soon.

I put the order in and sat more tables.

"I'm heading out with samples. Vito can read English, so give the orders to him," AJ said. "Gianna will handle drinks, and Rico will clear dirty dishes."

"Gotcha." AJ left, and the next customer walked in. It was the person I was waiting for—Eduardo Macelli from the bank. "Welcome back," I said.

He asked, "Is your *zia* here? I received the message to meet her."

"You did?" Of course he did—I'd left him the message to come here. "I think maybe there's been a mix-up, because she went to meet you at the bank," I said. "I'll call her on her cell phone." I knew Aunt Maria didn't have a cell phone. "Why don't you eat while you wait for her?" I was going to set him up with more than lunch.

"*Sì.*" He looked around the dining room. "Looks different," he said. "*Buono.*"

"Thanks. It's a work in progress." I hooked my arm into his. "You know, some of the glue on the chairs is still drying." I didn't even know if the chairs had any glue. "I hope you don't mind if I seat you with these two ladies just for a little while." Before Eduardo Macelli or the ladies could object, I dashed to get him fizzy water.

I remembered that Eduardo had liked the ricotta that I'd brought him yesterday. It wasn't a precise match with kalamata olives, but I had a feeling about this—bubbles in my gut. It felt right.

I told Gianna the drinks I needed. She pointed to Eduardo Macelli. "Why is he here?"

"So that he won't be at the bank when Aunt Maria gets there."

"Oh. Makes sense," she said.

"And who knows. Maybe he'll meet a lady," I added. I'd made a mental note yesterday that he wasn't wearing a wedding ring.

"Oh jeez," she said, and delivered the drinks.

When I returned with Eduardo Macelli's pizza, he and the two ladies were busily chatting about banking and football—that's soccer to you and me.

I continued to seat people in the newly decorated dining room.

A group of four giggly girls came in, holding white paper pie plates from AJ's sample tray. One said, "We're here for—" She hesitated.

"Pizza?" I asked.

"Our love match." They sounded American. Probably here for summer vacation or a school trip. She said, "The guy handing out samples told us to come here to meet the matchmaker." She glanced at the customers and asked me, "Can I get him?" She indicated a certain guy.

"Well, it doesn't really work that way," I explained. "What kind of pizza do you like?"

"That depends. What kind of pizza does *he* like?"

"He hasn't ordered yet, but I need to know your favorite kind in order to match you."

"*You're* the matchmaker?" she asked.

I nodded. "In the flesh."

"Huh. I thought you'd be an old lady with a crystal ball or something. You're not even Italian."

"Nah," I said. "More twenty-first century. And American matchmakers have come a long way since the Victorian era."

One of the girls, whose mouth was full of complicated orthodontic equipment, asked, "Why do you need to know our pizza?"

"It's just the way it works," I said. "What kind do you like?"

The first girl tapped each of her friends' shoulders one at a time, telling me their faves. "And Riley"—that was the girl with the braces—"she likes bacon, piled real high. And I just like mine plain."

"Well, in Rome we have an Italian bacon called pancetta. You'll love it," I said to Riley.

She smiled, revealing the metal.

I wrote down the orders. I already had a few ideas for three of the girls, but I didn't know what I was going to do with a pile of pancetta. I had never even dealt with regular American bacon. "Wait here," I said.

I walked around and looked at the pizza orders. I got a good feeling when I passed a table of four younger guys who all spoke English and looked like American tourists. I thought maybe I could match two of the girls. Fifty percent wasn't too bad for a beginner.

I pulled an empty table next to the boys' and said, "Hey there, I have a bit of an issue. I hope you can help me out. We just redecorated, and the tiles on the floor are loose in some places where we repositioned them. Do you mind if I put this table closer to yours so that no one trips?" I didn't let them answer. "Of course you don't mind. You look like nice guys." I pointed to one of them. "If you could just move down here to this chair—" The boys looked at each other, confused, but one of them started getting up. "Oh, not you." I pointed to a different guy. "You."

"Why me?" he asked.

"You have—um—a better—um—center of gravity. It will help equilibrate the tile sitch we've got, if you know what I mean."

"Gravity?"

"Yup. It's all about gravity. Am I right or am I right?" I rambled. "Very scientific."

One of them said, "Luke, dude, it's scientific. Just move."

Luke moved where I'd said.

"And you." I pointed to another one of them. "You sit here." He moved where I said. I waved to the girls to fill in the empty seats. "These girls have higher gravity and better—um—cerebellum. It's a girl thing, you wouldn't understand." Everyone got comfy. "Thank you all so, so much! You have no idea how helpful you've been." I scooted away before anyone could object.

AJ returned with his empty sample tray and helped Vito cook. This lunch was going well.

At one o'clock Murielle duPluie from the Rome newspaper walked in with a photographer on her heels.

She and I sat at the two-top (that's a table for two) near the door, so I could hear if any more matching requests came in.

She said, "I always record interviews so that I'm sure to get the quotes just right." She turned on a small tape recorder. "So tell me. How does this all work? The matches? And how did you get into this?"

"Well, I guess it all started because I like to be

around people. If I'm ever home alone, I walk down the street to visit my mom at the office where she works. It's next to a pizza place. She gives me money to get a slice. Sometimes I hang out there and watch people. I started to notice things about people and their pizza."

"Like what?"

"Like personality stuff."

"For example?"

"People who like everything on their pizza—I call them 'Everythings'—they're probably the easiest to describe. They're really outgoing, talkative, maybe a little loud."

"And who do these Everythings match with?" Murielle duPluie asked.

"Well, there are a few possibilities. I can't really reveal my secrets, if you know what I mean. Plus, it isn't an exact science."

"I understand. If you gave out all your formulas, anyone could be a Pizzeria Matchmaker."

"Too true. But it's not just the pizza. I get a certain, I don't know, like a feeling from people. When I mix that feeling with the pizza—KABOOM!—I make a match."

I saw her write "kaboom." "And you knew when I ordered that I would match well with Angelo?"

"I looked at the pizza options in the room and went

with my gut," I said. "When I mixed up your checks, it was sort of an experiment to see if there was a spark. I provided the intro, and you did the rest."

Just then I glanced over Murielle duPluie's shoulder to the window that looked out on the cobblestone street. Aunt Maria was coming back, earlier than planned.

Oh. No.

14

My thumb went to my ear, and I wiggled my fingers.

"Are you okay?" Murielle duPluie asked.

"Fine." I called, "Gi!" into the kitchen.

Gianna saw my signal and Aunt Maria. She raced to the door to intercept her. "I'm so glad you're here," she said to Aunt Maria. "Mmmm . . . errr . . ."

Gi, think fast.

"It's the sauce," Gianna blurted out.

Meanwhile, I pointed to the pictures hanging on the wall facing away from the door and said to Murielle duPluie, "Let me tell you a story about this picture right here. You'll love this, really."

I said, "That one is the house where this restaurant started."

I glanced over to Eduardo Macelli. He was in such deep conversation with the two ladies I'd sat him with that he didn't notice Aunt Maria.

I continued, "People came from all around. . . ." I heard Aunt Maria say, "*Mamma mia!* What is this about the sauce?" She hurried toward the kitchen without noticing Eduardo Macelli, the reporter, or someone taking my picture. That's how important sauce was to Aunt Maria.

AJ appeared with a stack of take-out containers. "You must be in a hurry," he said to Murielle duPluie and the photographer. "I wrapped up some tiramisu and rum cake for you guys to take with you." To me, so that Murielle duPluie could hear, he said, "We have a match-making request for you. High priority. A complicated case."

"Duty calls," I said.

Murielle duPluie looked at her watch. "Just one more question. What's *your* favorite topping?" she asked me.

I smiled. "Umm. I, umm . . . I like ham and pine-apple. But you really can't find that in Rome. It's an American thing."

"Maybe you can introduce it to Italy." She held her mic near AJ's mouth. "And you? What's yours?"

"I'm an anchovy guy. All the way. And you can quote me on that."

She smiled and asked me, "Is anchovy a good match with ham and pineapple?"

"That's more than one question," I said quickly. "I'll just say, 'Come to Amore Pizzeria, and maybe you'll find your love.'"

Murielle duPluie clicked off the recorder. "Thank you. *Merci*. This will be *formidable*. Maybe I can do a follow-up story in a few days and see how your skills are improving?"

"Sure." I led her to the front door. As she walked away, I listened to her stiletto heels *clickety-clack* down the cobblestones.

When she was a safe distance away, I spun around. "That was close," I said to AJ.

"You said 'duty,'" he said. "You know, like doody. Like poop."

Boys!

15

I flew into the kitchen. Aunt Maria was tasting the sauce. "It is perfect."

"Oh, phew," Gianna said. "I thought maybe it wasn't warm enough."

"Oh, you worry too much," Aunt Maria said. She looked at the dining room and saw Eduardo Macelli. "He here?"

"I know," I said. "If you had a cell phone, I could've called you to tell you."

"No cell phone." She went to talk to him. I held my

breath for a minute and watched them talk. They laughed, hopefully over the confusion of the meeting place.

When the lunch rush slowed down, Gianna and I sat at the corner near the register with one of Amore's menus. She had an assortment of glitter pens, stickers, and stampers. Meataball sat on the extra menus.

I studied menu items. There were so many wonderful traditional Italian dishes. I wondered if maybe Amore could add a few American-inspired pizzas. I wrote descriptions of three combos that I missed in Rome, while Gianna doodled around the edges.

"How about we name these after American cities?" I suggested. "This one will be the New York, this one the Philadelphia, and this one the Los Angeles."

"I love that idea. And I'll draw something from each city next to them—the Empire State Building, the Liberty Bell, and the Hollywood sign."

The new menu was going to look great and offer some items that no other pizzeria in the area had.

"So," Gianna began. "Rico's cute."

"Sure," I said.

"You know, it doesn't make sense to me that you're a matchmaker, yet you've never had a match of your own," Gianna continued. "I mean, shouldn't the matchmaker have some experience in romance?"

"Umm . . . maybe. I guess." Hm. I'd never really thought about it that way.

"Maybe this could be the summer that you have your first love?" Gianna teased.

I rolled my eyes. Saving Aunt Maria's shop and making matches were stressful enough—I didn't need any more drama in the kitchen!

16

Aunt Maria usually unlocked the Amore Pizzeria door at eleven o'clock in the morning. But the next day, when we were sweeping up the dining room from the work done on the walls the night before, we watched customers begin to gather out front at ten thirty.

"Who are all these people?" she asked. "Are they here because of your samples?"

"I guess so," I said. "They were really good. After all, they have your sauce." I tucked Aunt Maria's copy of *Il Messaggero* with Murielle duPluie's article under the counter where I kept my matchmaking notes, which were growing to a nice size.

Aunt Maria called to AJ and Vito, "You have some crust rolled out? I open the doors early."

"Yup," AJ said.

"Okay." She asked me, "You can ask Gianna, Jane, and Rico to come down and help?"

I took the broom to the back corner of the store and knocked on the ceiling four times.

Knock—knock—knock—knock.

It was followed by four stomps. A minute later Gianna, Jane, and Rico walked in the back door.

"What's up?" Gianna asked.

Aunt Maria said, "We need the help today." She pointed to the customers.

Rico said, "Food service is not really my gig." He pushed a button on the copper espresso machine and watched hot brown liquid drip into a tiny ceramic cup. Then he leaned on the counter and sipped it. "I'll be your support system."

"What is 'gig'?" Aunt Maria took an apron off a hook and wrapped it around his waist. It was long, crisp, and white. She handed him a pad and pen. "There. You are the waiter. Gianna, you are the hostess. AJ, you are the assistant cook. Lucy, the waitress. Everybody has a job. Now, *andiamo.* Let's Go!"

Rico huffed and took his last sip of espresso.

"Just smile a lot," Gianna said to him. "You'll be fine."

I said to Gianna, "Let's check out those new votive candles you put in the dining room." And I tugged her arm.

"What?" she asked. "I can see them from here. They're fine. But just look at that wall." She pointed to the one that had been scraped with a wire brush last night. It revealed the original brick but still left speckles of white in the grooves. The result was a beautiful old-world feel that really captured traditional Rome and the personality of Amore Pizzeria. "It's more fab than I'd imagined it could be."

"I know," I said. "I just want us to have a plan for the matching."

"You're gonna keep doing it?"

"Look." I pointed to the crowd outside the door. "That's why they're here. I can't let them down." I added, "It's for the good of Amore Pizzeria."

She sighed. "What do I have to do?"

I thought for a moment.

"Put people looking for matches on this half of the dining room. That'll be my half. Rico can wait on the other half."

"Fine. You know Aunt Maria is going to be mad when she finds out about all of this."

"But she's happy about all the customers. Maybe she'll be happy and mad," I said. "Then I'll tell her how hungry I am, and I'll just eat and eat. That will make her more happy than mad."

"Probably."

My section of the restaurant filled up quickly. I took orders and studied customers. Some of the matches jumped out at me right away, and some were more complicated.

I delivered sausage to a woman and called out, "Who ordered the garlic?" A man yelled in Italian, but I figured he was claiming the garlic. "Come over here." I set the garlic plate next to the sausage. "You two enjoy your lunch." They giggled and shook hands.

"Who has sliced zucchini?"

A girl raised her hand.

"Come on over here and sit with this gentleman."

This was the way I made the matches, by moving people around. I watched the customers and took notes on an extra order pad. When I finished, I stashed it under the register. I didn't know if I'd made true love matches, but lots of people looked happy. Obviously, they all loved their pizza.

Aunt Maria came out from the kitchen and manned the cash register as customers left.

"How was your lunch?" Maria asked the sausage customer.

"It was great," she said.

"And the pizza was delicious too," the man who ordered garlic added.

Gianna glanced at her phone. A huge grin crossed her face, and she hunched over in the corner as she thumbed a message. I had a pretty good idea who she was texting.

When she returned to her job, she sat a table in Rico's section, where a waiter who I'd never seen took their order and gave it to AJ. I found Rico sitting at a table, sipping an espresso.

"What are you doing?" I asked him.

"What? You mean that guy? He's a friend of mine." He shrugged. "And he has some serving experience."

Aunt Maria rang up one of the last customers and caught my eye with a menacing glare. Then she stuck out her finger and bent it in, like, *Come here.*

Gulp.

She looked way mad, like, angry with a side of enraged.

I smiled. "I'm starving."

"We talk."

"Can I eat first? I think I'm gonna pass out."

"Fine. Get some food and come right back."

In the kitchen AJ said to me, "She looks pretty angry."

"No duh," I said. "Can you make me a meatball sandwich?"

"One sec. I'm outta sauce." He put the empty pot in a pile of dirty dishes and lifted another simmering pot from the back to the front burner. Then he scooped three lovely meatballs onto crusty Italian bread and covered it with the sauce from the new pot. "Cheese?"

"Why in the world would anyone eat a meatball sandwich without cheese?" I asked. "Do you know the only thing that goes better than cheese?"

"What's that?"

"More cheese!"

He smiled. "Toasted?"

"Put 'er in."

He slid the pan with my sandwich into the oven. It took only a few Mississippis for the cheese to melt.

I took my plate back to the cash register with Aunt Maria and braced myself to be yelled at in Italian.

"Want a bite?" I asked her.

"No." She held up the newspaper. There was a picture of me. The headline read, MATCHMAKER AT AMORE PIZZERIA.

"Look. I'm sorry. I know you said not to. You said,

'*Capisce?*' But then that reporter came in. I matched her the other day as an experiment. And that went really well. She wanted to do an article. She said it would be good for business. And I love you so much and love Amore Pizzeria so much that I couldn't let—"

She held up her hand for me to stop talking.

A few beats later, she broke into a huge smile. Then she pushed a button on the cash register and the drawer flew open. It was full of money. "It worked!"

"So you're not mad?"

"I'm furious. But I'm so happy." She hugged me. "You eat!"

I was just about to sink my teeth into the sandwich when a customer yelled, "Water! *Acqua!*" He grabbed a glass and chugged it, half of it spilling down the front of his shirt. "That sauce! It's too spicy! Are you trying to kill me?"

The sauce?

I touched the sauce on my sandwich with my tongue. "Yowww! He's right," I said to Aunt Maria, and grabbed my own glass of water.

Aunt Maria yelled to AJ, "Where did that pot come from?"

AJ said, "The walk-in fridge. It's the batch you made Wednesday."

She looked at the bubbling pot, grabbed a spoon, and tasted the sauce. She immediately spit it out.

"Someone has ruined my sauce," Aunt Maria yelled. "Who would do that?"

17

"Mamma mia!" Aunt Maria shouted. "What happened to the sauce?"

AJ said, "I'll take the extra pot out of the fridge and pop it on the stove."

"Do not 'pop' anything," said Aunt Maria. "Just heat it."

"That's what I meant," AJ said.

"Then do not say 'pop.' I no understand you kids anymore."

AJ retreated to the kitchen, while Gianna told the customer that we were making a new lunch for him.

"The sitch isn't that bad," I said to Aunt Maria, who was now fanning herself with an empty drink tray. "We didn't make any pizza with that sauce yet."

"'Sitch'?" Aunt Maria shook her head. "Is good we have the extra pot, but that will change the sauce-making schedule. We will run out before Wednesday."

"We'll make more! You can teach me."

"*Sì!* But I need very special ingredients. I go all over Rome to get only the best. It takes time. A lot of places. A lot of time," she said. "Without the ingredients, I cannot teach you."

I looked at my watch. "I'll go after lunch. Give me a list of what you need and addresses."

"You do not know Rome. You will not find these places."

I held up my phone. "I have GPS. It works in Rome."

She looked at my phone and shook her head. "'Gee peas'? No. You go with Rico. He can follow the map. You know a map?"

"Yes, I know what a map is."

We looked at Rico sipping another espresso, and Aunt Maria added, "You two cannot carry everything. I make many trips. AJ and Gianna will go too." Then she waved to Jane, who came over with her arms filled with dirty dishes. "Can you stay with me? I need the help for dinner."

"Absolutely," Jane said. "Anything you need."

Rico's waiter guy lingered nearby and called over to us, "I'll help too."

"Who that?" Aunt Maria asked, confused.

"Does it matter?" I asked. "He knows what he's doing, and he wants to stay and help."

"Okay." Aunt Maria pointed at him. "You stay."

He asked, "And I can call *mio amico*?"

"*Sì*," Aunt Maria said to his offer to call a friend.

"What if people come in for matches?" I asked her. "I'll show you the notes I've been taking."

"You no worry," she said. "It is under control."

18

When the lunch crowd thinned, the four of us headed out with the list and instructions that directed us to three very different areas of Rome for garlic, herbs, and tomatoes.

Rico's waiter friend let us use his scooter, so Gianna and I hopped on it while AJ and Rico got on AJ's.

"Do you know how to drive that?" AJ asked me.

"No," I said. "But how hard could it be?"

Rico got off the scooter with AJ and said to me, "Let's switch. You go with AJ and I'll drive this one."

I sat behind AJ. Gianna raised her brows at me

because I was sitting so close to a boy. She motioned for me to wrap my arms around his waist, but I was unsure. . . .

AJ put a helmet on my head and secured it under my chin. Then he hit the gas hard—I almost fell off the back—so I grabbed his waist and held on for my life. It wasn't as weird as I'd thought. Actually, I kind of liked it.

We followed Rico and Gianna.

Gianna filled Rico's ear with chatter and pointed to everything. I was content to look around and take it all in. The sun was warm on my back, and the breeze felt cool on my cheeks. I was surprised at the women on scooters—dressed up, even in spiky heels—with bread and flowers in their baskets. Men also scootered around in suits and ties. My mind spun stories about many of these people, and I wondered if they were looking for matches.

I could've ridden around all day, imagining, but we soon arrived at our first stop.

Garlic.

"Where are we?" Gianna hooked her helmet to the back of the scooter.

I pointed. "That's the Pantheon, Gi. It's kinda famous."

"Oh sure," she said. "I knew that."

I rolled my eyes.

Rico unfolded the paper Aunt Maria had given us. "Well, we're at the Piazza della Rotonda. According to Maria, there's a street vendor who sits next to the water-ice stand that sells *fragola*. That's strawberry. He should have her garlic."

"Why not just get it from a store?" Gianna asked.

AJ said, "Oh, no. She is very specific with her sauce. Everything comes from a vendor she knows and trusts. She's been going to the same places for years. It's one of the things that makes her sauce perfect. The garlic comes from a family that grows it in their yard. It's the only thing they sell. She says there's something about their soil that makes it more pungent than anyone else's."

I was totally gonna use that little deet in a story. "That's awesome," I said. In my mind I pictured a cottage in the country and an old gray-haired Italian man picking carefully selected cloves.

I scanned the piazza and easily counted four water-ice vendors, all next to people selling some kind of herbs or vegetables. "This could take a while. We better split up."

AJ said, "And look for clues?"

"What clues?" I asked.

"Like Scooby-Doo. They always split up and look for clues."

We ignored him—although I thought it was funny—and each of us ran to a different vendor. On the way to mine I stopped to eavesdrop on a tour group. Their leader said, "The columns are made of granite. They were floated down the Nile, then the Tiber River, before being dragged here. When you see columns in the US, they were inspired by these."

I wanted to hear more, but . . . the garlic.

I waited in line at the water-ice vendor's cart. When it was my turn, I looked at the ground and mumbled, "*Fragola?*"

He shook his head. "*Limone. Caffè.*" He didn't have strawberry.

"*Grazie,*" I thanked him.

On my way back to our agreed meeting place, I lingered again by the tour. The guide said, "It was originally a temple to worship Roman gods, and then it became a church. It's also a tomb."

Oh, how I love a good tomb story.

The guide continued, "That huge dome has an ocular—an opening that looks into the sky. It's quite magnificent. Let's get our tickets and go see."

I wanted to see. I thought maybe I could blend in and tag along, but . . . the garlic.

Rico and Gianna were waiting. I showed them my

empty hands. All our hope was pinned on AJ, who came back with four red granitas. He handed them out.

"*Fragola*," he said. "Strawberry for everyone."

I took my cup and tasted it with a little plastic spoon. It was finely grated ice shavings covered with strawberry flavoring. "What about the garlic?"

AJ took a paper bag out of his back pocket. "I got your garlic, girl," he said with strawberry-red lips.

He concentrated on his ice, then asked, "It's good, huh? Sometimes I eat it really fast to get a brain freeze."

"You do that to yourself on purpose?" Rico asked.

AJ looked shocked. "You don't?"

The ice was good, but we were in a hurry. Aunt Maria wanted us back at Amore Pizzeria before dark. She said the sauce would take about six hours. I can't imagine something taking SIX hours to cook. I looked at my watch. "We better get going. What's next? Tomatoes?"

Rico had a big blob of ice on his tongue, which he tried to talk through. "It's near the Colosseum. Not far."

We finished most of our ices, hopped back on the scooters, and headed toward Aunt Maria's tomato supplier. On the way, we crossed another piazza with a grand fountain. This one was chock-full of kids splashing around. A few adults, too—they'd rolled up their pants legs and waded in to cool off.

Large tents lined the square, filled with anything and everything you could think of: shoes, sundresses, jewelry, paintings, oil, flowers, cheese, fruit, and vegetables. If we weren't racing to get tomatoes, I totally would've shopped.

As I glanced around, I saw the Colosseum from a distance. The first thing that struck me was its size. It was massive, like a huge, ancient, crumbling stone football stadium. The second thing I thought was how strange it was that this ruin was right there in the middle of a city. The crumbling building was surrounded by a busy street, people taking pictures and buying souvenirs from men in red gladiator robes and helmets topped with Mohawk brushes.

I turned my head to make sure I didn't miss seeing another timeworn treasure.

That's when I saw something—well, someone—that surprised me.

Lorenzo.

19

~

I whipped my head around and said to AJ, "Lorenzo's following us."

He tilted his head, confused. I repeated myself louder, but got the same reaction. That probably meant that Rico hadn't heard anything that Gianna had been saying. *Ha!*

When we parked, I took off my helmet, fluffed my hair, and casually scanned the area, which was crowded with Colosseum viewers.

"Don't look now," I said to AJ, Rico, and Gianna, "but Lorenzo is behind us."

Rico moved the scooter's side mirror so he could check. "Yup," he said. "It's hard to hide that huge head of hair."

AJ said, "If I didn't think he was such a jerk, I might be jealous of it."

Gianna added, "It is kind of fab." And she sighed. I think she really had a thing for him, which wasn't good, since in my book, he was suspect numero uno in the sauce sitch, if you know what I mean.

I guess I was the only one not in love with Lorenzo's hair. "Can we forget about the hair for a minute? Is anyone wondering why he's following us?" I asked. Without letting anyone answer, I said, "I think I smell something."

"It wasn't me," AJ protested.

"That's not what I meant," I snapped. "I think that batch of sauce was sabotaged."

"And you think it was Lorenzo?" Rico asked.

"He was alone in the kitchen," I pointed out.

"How do you know that?" Gianna asked.

Rico said, "It's amazing what you can learn when you're crouched on the floor in Jane Attilio's apartment."

Gianna asked, "What? Crouched?"

AJ said, "Don't worry, I don't get it either."

Gianna finally realized what we meant. "You listened to my private conversation?" she shrieked.

"You let Lorenzo in the kitchen," I said defensively. "Pizzeria de Roma is Amore's biggest competition. Don't you think that was, like, a bad idea?"

AJ said, "Whoa. Stop right there. He was in Maria's kitchen? Lorenzo?" He threw his hands up in frustration. "He would totally ruin the sauce."

"No way," Gianna said. She tilted the scooter's mirror to catch a glimpse of him. She studied him for a second. "You think?"

"Totes," I assured her. "And I think he's following us to find out where Maria gets her stuff."

"Or maybe he's following me," Gianna said.

I loved her optimism, but she just wasn't being realistic. "Don't worry," I said. "We'll get back at him."

AJ asked, "Like, how? Are we talking about food contamination? Or maybe give them a little cockroach infestation? A health code violation? A huge 'closed for renovation' sign?"

"Your mind is way more creative, and scarily sinister, than I'd ever imagined," I said to AJ.

"Really, dude," Rico said. "Remind me not to make you mad."

"So, what's the plan?" Gianna asked.

"It's brewing," I assured them. "You leave that to me. We'll get him when he least expects it."

"Cool." AJ looked at his watch. "But right now we need to track down some tomatoes. Or is it tom-ah-toes?"

No one answered his question.

Rico unfolded the paper with instructions and looked around. "They're there." He pointed to a nearby open-air market.

"But Lorenzo will see where we get them," I said. "He'll try to copy Aunt Maria's sauce."

"Fret not, Pizzeria Matchmaker, I'll take care of that," Rico said. "You get"—he checked the paper—"a hundred tomatoes."

"I'm on it," I said. I ran about two steps, then turned back to Rico. "Don't actually injure him."

"I wouldn't dream of it," Rico said. Then to Gianna, he said, "You're helping me."

"I am? I don't know; that's not really my style."

"Make it your style," I said. "This is kinda your fault. Aunt Maria told you to stay away from him."

"She also told you to 'no mess with the love,'" Gianna said.

"True, but that hasn't been a disaster," I said.

"Yet," she added, and left with Rico.

I hoped that wasn't true.

AJ asked me, "What do you want me to do?"

"Stay here and guard the garlic," I said. "If you see

me do this"—I flapped my arms like a bird—"that means I need help with the tom-ah-toes."

"So, I'm your wingman?" he asked.

"If that's what you wanna call it. Sure."

"I'm calling it that," AJ confirmed.

Maybe I should tell you what my opinion was of AJ at this point. I liked him. Not *liked* liked (well, maybe a little). I thought he was a fun wingman to have around. But if those tomatoes grew feet, organized into an army, and started taking over the planet, I don't know that I would want him in my rebel troop. I didn't think he could handle a serious zombie tomato event.

Zombie tom-ah-toes? Now, that was an idea for a story.

20

I found the vegetable stand in the outdoor market where Rico had directed me. The tomatoes looked red and ripe and without the slightest hint of coming to life with a desire to take over the planet.

"*Buongiorno*," a woman wearing a short black apron with pockets said. "I help you with something?"

"*Sì*. I am Lucia Rossi, Maria's niece. She sent me to get tomatoes for her."

"Ah, *sì*. You are early this week. She was just here."

"Right. I know. We had a little sitch—situation."

She looked at me like she didn't understand.

"You see, my sister Gianna, she likes this boy. The kind that she shouldn't like, if you know what I mean. And, well, she let him into the kitchen of all places, and—"

The woman stared at me blankly. She didn't follow what I was saying. "You know what?" I asked. "Never mind. I'll just take a hundred tomatoes."

She hoisted a jug onto the table and then another, and another and two more. Four.

"What's that?" I asked.

"For Maria, I peel and crush. Always I peel and"— she smashed her fist into her palm, like, really hard— "crush."

Now, *that's* a woman I'd want in my rebel army troop.

"Gotcha. A lot of crushing." I looked at the jugs. Now I knew why Aunt Maria had sent all four of us. I couldn't carry all this. I stepped out into the open space and flapped my arms, but my wingman was nowhere to be found.

Grrr.

The tomato woman looked at me. "You okay?"

"*Sì.*" I took two of the jugs. "I'll come back for those."

"No problem," she said.

I carried one in each arm. Man, they were heavy.

How did Aunt Maria do this? She must've had some kind of system. "Oh." I turned back to the woman. "What do I owe you?"

"You no worry. Maria never need to pay with me."

I nodded.

Then she asked, "You don't have the case?"

"Case of what?"

"Maria, she put the tomatoes in a—" She made a motion with her hands like a big square. "It has a hand-hold, and she pull it on the wheels." She pointed to the jugs. "Too heavy to carry like that."

No duh.

"Box with a handhold, huh?" I set the jugs down and looked around the market. "Gimme a minute, please."

"Sure. You have one minute, two minute, as many minute as you want."

I walked around to the various vendors. I smelled leather and oil, even though I saw neither.

"*Acqua?*" a man selling bottles of water asked me. He kept the bottles in a cooler with a handle that slid out to roll it along.

I looked into it. He only had three bottles left, I guess because it was late in the day. "Can I have all three bottles?" I asked.

"*Si!*" He seemed excited to sell out.

"And your cooler, too?"

"This?" He pointed to the cooler. "No. No. Not for sale."

I reached into the back of my pocket. "How about five euros?"

"No. No." He shook his head.

"How about ten euros?"

"No." He considered. "Fifteen euros?"

"Deal," I said, and *BAM!* I had a way to get the jugs to Aunt Maria's without my arms falling off.

I rolled it behind me, loaded the jugs, and returned to the scooters, where AJ stood eating a *panino*.

"Seriously? You left your wingman for a sandwich?"

He looked at the sandwich. "Sorry." Then he said, "I thought I was the wingman."

"You're mine and I'm yours. We're each other's wingman. That's the way it works."

"Really?" AJ asked. "You think?"

"Yeah, I do."

He looked at the cooler. "What's that?"

"One hundred tomatoes. Peeled and"—I smashed my fist into my palm—"crushed."

"Sweet." He bit the *panino*. "You want a bite?"

"I guess."

. . .

By the time Rico and Gianna returned, laughing, AJ and I had lifted the cooler onto the back of one of the scooters and secured it.

"What's so funny?" I asked.

"You should've seen how Rico distracted Lorenzo," Gianna said.

"That dude is such an idiot," Rico said. "I blew cherry pits through a straw and pegged him right in the face." He laughed so hard he could hardly get the words out. "I was hiding, and he was looking all around, like 'What was that?' And he ran in our direction, but we had moved."

Gianna said, "When he got to the place where we had been, Rico blew another from a totally different spot."

"Then we split up and pegged him from two sides. He didn't know what to do with that," Rico added. To Gianna he said, "I swear you've done that before. Your aim was on the money."

"First time, I swear."

"Where is he now?" I asked.

"He took off," Rico said. "I don't think we have to worry about him anymore today."

"Today," I repeated. "What about the rest of the week?"

"What's your plan to get even with him?" AJ asked.

"The details are still coming together in my head," I said. "This type of genius takes careful consideration, but it's gonna be good."

21

⚛

"To the Piazza di Spagna and the Spanish Steps," Rico said, starting up his scooter, the back end of which sagged due to a cooler with four heavy jugs of crushed tomatoes.

He gave us a forward wave and rode off. Slowly.

The other motorists honked at us, and a few yelled. Luckily, I couldn't understand their Italian. Slow was not the Italian way of driving. A group of teen boys on bicycles chuckled as they pedaled past us.

I had come here to the Spanish Steps the last time I was in Rome, but that was such a long time ago that

I hardly remembered. The Piazza di Spagna was huge and very crowded. The Fontana della Barcaccia sat in the middle of the piazza. People of all ages sat on the edge of the fountain, sipping coffee or eating granitas or gelato with little plastic spoons. Shopping bags from Fendi, Prada, and Gucci sat on the ground next to them.

Behind the fountain was a grand staircase—I mean it was *HUGE*, and beautiful. I didn't count, but it looked like more than a hundred massive stone steps. At the top was an ancient church. Flowers—pots of colorful violets and daisies—lined the steps on either side.

Ladies in flowing skirts, carrying baskets filled with long-stemmed red roses, strolled up and down the steps. When they saw a couple posing for a photograph, one of the ladies would encourage the man to buy a rose for his date.

"We have to go up there." Rico pointed to the top of the steps. "There are shops. One of them sells herbs."

As I followed Rico up the steps, I was totally overcome with déjà vu. You know the feeling like you've been somewhere or done something before? Well, I had actually been here before, but it was more than that—I felt like I had been here before *with Rico*. And as fast as the feeling came, it left.

AJ and Gianna walked up too. Our climbing was

interrupted by a woman selling roses from a basket. "For your girlfriend?" she asked AJ.

"Oh, she's not my girlfriend. She's a friend."

The woman said, "And she's a girl. So, she is your girlfriend. Buy her a flower."

"Um . . . er . . . um." AJ couldn't form a single non-mumbled word.

"No, thanks," I said.

We caught up to Rico and Gianna, who were taking a rose from a different woman. I imagined Rico couldn't say "No, thanks" either, and Gianna probably really wanted the rose.

The woman handed one to me.

"No, thanks," I said again.

"Oh, you take this. You are Maria Rossi's niece, sì? You must have a rose."

"How did you know that?" I asked.

"It's all she's talked about for days, and you look just like her."

I took the rose. "What do we owe you?"

"Nothing. I'd do anything for Maria."

"Wow. Thanks." I wondered what Aunt Maria had done for her.

"I am Carina." She shook my hand.

"Hi. I'm—"

"Lucy. I know. I hope you have a wonderful visit." She turned to another customer after saying "*Ciao*" to us.

We made it to the top of the steps and found the shop that had the herbs for the sauce. Thankfully, herbs were much lighter than jugs of crushed tomatoes. Then we headed back to Amore Pizzeria, with the tomato jugs weighing us down. After safely tucking the coveted ingredients way in the back of the walk-in fridge, we all helped with the few remaining dinner customers.

"Do you need me to, you know . . . make any matches?" I asked Aunt Maria.

I followed her eyes to the dining room. "Is all taken care of," she said.

There were couples holding hands, giggling, smiling, and exchanging phone numbers.

"How did you do that?" I asked her. "How did you know who to match with who? I didn't ever show you my notes."

She rang up two customers at the cash register. "*Grazie*," she said to them. They walked down the cobblestone alley arm in arm.

"The notes do not matter. Is not like sauce. There is no recipe you can follow," she said. "It is a feeling. A gift."

"Matchmaking is a gift?" I asked.

Aunt Maria smiled. "*Sì*, one that runs in the family. You aren't the only one who knows the matchmaking."

120

22

I couldn't believe it. "Whoa! You can do it too?"

She laughed. "Yes, I can."

"That is, like, cool with a side of oh yeah!"

"Right. 'Cool,'" she said. "Yeah."

"I can't believe this! Why didn't you tell me sooner?" I asked.

"Meddling in matters of love is big responsibility. Some matches go wrong. I know this."

"But lots go right." I pointed to the backs of the couple who had walked out a minute ago.

"Oh, I know. I make many, many good matches, but then I stop."

"Why?"

She looked at the clock. "For another day," she said, and reached under the counter. "But look at this." It was a basket with three envelopes.

"What are those?"

"Letters from people asking the Pizzeria Matchmaker for help," she said. "They think you are the new Beatrice."

"Who's Beatrice?"

"I tell you the story later. You are not the only one who can tell the story. That run in the family too."

"We have a lot to talk about," I said.

"*Sì*. We will talk while we make the sauce."

Then she pulled a large piece of laminated paper from under the cash register. "Salvatore the deliveryman leave this here on the counter today." She handed it to me.

"The happy guy who brings meat and bread? He brings menus, too?"

"*Sì*. Salvatore. He bring everything. That is the job of the deliveryman."

"I guess," I said. I thought it was a little strange that he would deliver pasta *and* menus—very different things.

She pointed to an item on the menu—the New York—that I had added. "What is this?"

"It's great," I said. "I'll show you how to make it."

"I hope you will. Now, we better start on the sauce. It take six hours." Aunt Maria announced, "No big dinner tonight. Me and Lucy, we make the sauce. We will eat while we clean up."

I followed her into the kitchen.

Vito had a big pot of leftover spaghetti. He put some on a plate and cut it up for Meataball, then made a plate for himself.

I took a round roll and hollowed out the soft middle. Then I filled it with spaghetti, sauce, and mozzarella cheese. I set the other half of the roll on top and pushed down.

"What you doing?" Aunt Maria asked.

"It's a spaghetti Parmesan sandwich. I made it up." I took a bite.

"Mamma mia."

"It's good." I handed it to her, and she took a bite.

"Sì. It is good," she agreed. I think she was surprised she liked it!

I made one for everyone.

AJ bit into his. "It's the perfect way to take spaghetti on the go. The only thing that would be better would be if we could put it on a stick."

I thought about this while I cleaned. Spaghetti on a stick? Good idea! Could it be done?

With everyone helping, it didn't take long to reset the dining room for lunch tomorrow.

Aunt Maria waved her arms. "You are all done with the cleanup. *Grazie*. Now, you go. Lucy and I have to work." She shoved everyone out the door.

The gang left. Aunt Maria locked the door behind them and turned off the lights except for the kitchen. "Get the ingredients."

I did as directed while Aunt Maria lifted a huge metal pot akin to a cauldron onto the stove. She slid a little step stool over so that she could get high enough to see inside the pot.

She poured in olive oil without measuring and put the burner on low-medium while she showed me how to use a garlic press.

She said, "You put the garlic in the oil." She waited for me to press seven cloves and add them to the oil. I added it carefully and snapped my arm back when the garlic popped and sizzled.

"Now you stir." She took a very long silver spoon off a hook on the wall. "Only this spoon."

"How come? Does it have some special Italian magical power?"

"Always with the story, you are," Aunt Maria said. "It is the spoon I always use to make the sauce, and the sauce is always good, so that is the way to make it."

"My explanation is much more interesting."

"Sì," she said. "But just a story."

We carefully worked through the rest of the secret recipe, adding tomatoes and herbs. She measured nothing, and I wasn't allowed to write anything down. "That is how it stay a secret. It is here." She pointed to her head.

"How do you know you're getting it right if you don't measure?"

"You taste every time. Your taste know if it is right." She took a plastic spoon and touched the garlic and oil with it. She let it cool for a sec, then let me lick it. "Close your eyes. This is how it should taste right now." She paused. "Remember it."

I wasn't confident I was going to remember, so I concentrated.

Aunt Maria threw the spoon away and continued her sauce routine.

"You have a lot to tell me," I said. "What's with this family 'gift' that I seem to have inherited from you? You know, I always thought there was something special connecting us."

"I did too." She pinched my cheek.

"How did it start?" I asked her.

125

"I was making the pizza." She pointed into the dining room to the picture on the wall. "Right there."

I nodded and continued to slowly stir with the silver spoon and commit the details of the recipe to memory while listening.

"I was young and married to Ferdinando. My lady friends were not married. They would come over for the pizza. Ferdinando's friends would come over for the pizza too. I started getting ideas in my head about the pizzas they liked and a feeling in my heart about which lady would match well with which man."

"That's exactly what happens to me."

"The matches, they worked." She used the tips of her fingers to sprinkle sugar in the bubbling red liquid, stirred, and dabbed a bit on the end of a plastic spoon for me to taste. "Remember that," she said about the taste. "Sometimes you need a little more sugar, sometimes less."

I tried to memorize the taste—not as easy as it sounds.

"The matches is how we got the name Amore Pizzeria. *Amore* is love in Italian," she said. "Everyone loved the matches."

"Then what happened? How come you 'no mess with love' anymore?"

"Because of a bad match I made. I paired a woman with a man, and they go off to America. Then I met another man who I just know is the perfect match for her, but she is gone." A sad look came over her face. "He never marry. I always see him and he so sad. I think this is my fault. I feel so guilty, I stop the matching."

Everything had been added to the pot. Aunt Maria turned the heat down and stirred the deep-red liquid with a long wooden spoon. "Now, we let it simmer."

2 3

Dear Pizzeria Matchmaker: I like pepperoni pizza. I'm coming into Amore tomorrow. Please make a match for me.

Dear "Beatrice": Please help me find my true love. From Kelsey

Dear Beatrice II: Please make me a match. Love, Basil and Tomato

Cara Beatrice: Voglio incontrare il mio vero
amore. Da Bianca

I piled the four new letters on top of the old ones. AJ rolled out dough. "What are you going to do with those?"

"I'm not sure yet," I said. "I don't even know anything about Beatrice. Aunt Maria was supposed to tell me about it last night, but we got so preoccupied with matchmaking that we didn't have time. Do you know she does it too?"

"Matchmaking?"

I nodded and helped spread sauce on the dough. "Well, she used to, but not anymore."

"How come?"

"She made a bad match and felt so guilty about it that she swore she wouldn't do it after that."

"Oh man, that's heavy stuff," AJ said.

"Yeah. I don't know how I would feel if a match I made went bad. I mean, should a matchmaker really be responsible for what happens after the intro?"

"*That*, Lucy, is a question for a matchmaker, which is your department," AJ said. "I roll dough. You make matches. It works for us."

I sighed. "I don't know." I wiped my hands on a towel and picked up the small pile of letters. "I guess I'll just hang on to these for now. What did Beatrice do with them?"

"Well, she was dead when she started getting letters, so I don't think there really was much she *could* do with them." He slid the crusts into the oven. "How can you be Italian and not know about Beatrice and Dante?"

"Well, I don't. So tell me."

"It's a love story," he said, and made a face, like love was gross. "Beatrice Portinari lived in Florence about a bajillion years ago. As a child she met Dante at a party. For Dante it was love at first sight. Supposedly, they wrote letters to each other for many years."

"How romantic. No one does that anymore. Maybe a text sometimes."

"Whatever," he said. "Eventually they each married other people, but it is said that Dante always loved her."

"And they reunited?"

"No," he said. "She died, remember?"

"Oh, that's a terrible ending," I said.

"Blahbity blah," he said. "But there's more."

"Well, don't keep me waiting. Bring it on," I said.

"In Florence there is a tomb for Beatrice. Letters started mysteriously appearing. They asked Beatrice, or her ghost or spirit or whatever, for help finding love."

"People think I'm Beatrice?" I said. "Like, reincarnated? Or back from the dead?"

"It's more likely that they think you're *like* Beatrice," AJ said. "Maybe that you can help with their romantic needs."

"But a modern version," I added. "What does the dead Beatrice do for them?"

"I don't know. Maybe makes their wishes come true, I guess. Like a wish in a fountain."

I looked at the letters. "I can't make wishes come true. I'm not a magician. If they think I am, I'm going to disappoint a lot of people," I said. "It's just pizza and a feeling in my gut."

"I guess they'll take whatever they can get."

"What do you think I should do with these?" I indicated the letters in my hand. "They don't have addresses, so replying isn't an option."

He tied a bandanna around his head and headed toward the walk-in refrigerator. "I bet you'll think of something."

I was left wondering about a lot of matchmaker-y things and something else. The Beatrice and Dante story was bothering me, and I wasn't sure why.

AJ had propped the refrigerator door open and

called out to me, "We'll go to the Festa de Santa Elizabeth tomorrow night and take your mind off it for a while."

"What's that?"

He brought out a crate of cheese and sifted through it. "It's only one of the biggest, funnest summer events in Rome. It's a street festival that lasts all night. There's food and dancing and music. It's a total blast," he said. "If there was a place like that where we could go every night, that would be awesome."

"Sounds great. But won't we have to work?" I asked.

"Nah. All the businesses close. Everyone will be at the Festa."

"If there really was a place like that all the time, no one would ever work," I said.

"I guess, or maybe then it would be more usual," AJ said. "You know, like, normal and not such a big deal."

"Maybe," I said. "Well, it sounds like fun."

"Oh, it is."

"What should I wear?"

"That's really more Rico's department. Besides, we've got customers."

I could tell by the smirks on the women's faces that they were looking for more than pizza.

"Table for two?" I asked them.

"Yes. And two matches, please."

No one else was here for lunch yet, but they would be soon. I sat them smack-dab in the middle of the dining room, thinking that would give me lots of options.

"Tell me about your pizza. What do you like?"

One of the women said, "Roasted vegetables."

The other said, "Mushroom."

Mushroom was easy peasy, but roasted vegetables? I didn't have an immediate idea in mind. I went to grab my notepad.

I kept it under the register, but when I went over, it wasn't there. I looked on the counter, near the bar, on the ledge between the dining room and kitchen.

It was gone.

24

I hustled into the kitchen and found Meataball keeping AJ company while he moved stuff around in the walk-in refrigerator. "Have you seen my matchmaking notepad?"

"It was under the register."

"It's not there now."

"Dunno," he said. "Can you do it without your notes?"

"I guess I don't have much of a choice."

I sat more customers, and soon I had a selection of men to choose from: pepperoni, plain, basil, and jala- peño peppers.

I'd never worked with jalapeños before, so I left him out.

"I've matched basil and mushroom before. It's a tried-and-true combo, but what about the lady with roasted vegetables?"

"What is your gut telling you?" AJ asked.

"Strangely, it's telling me jalapeño."

"Then go with it."

"What if it's a disaster?" I asked.

"You won't know until you try," he said. "It might not be."

"I guess," I said. "Let me know if you see my notes."

"Will do."

I switched the customers' seats around. Then I watched and waited. Right away I could tell something was up with mushroom and basil. The woman's face grew redder with each passing minute, and as I delivered her pizza, she tossed her Coke in Mr. Basil's face. He jumped up and yelled, "What? Are you crazy?"

She looked at me. "You are a terrible Pizzeria Matchmaker, and I'm going to tell everyone." She slid her phone out of her purse and tapped the screen. "There. It's posted. Now everyone knows you're a fraud." She stormed to the door.

"Wait," I said. "I'm sorry. Let me try again."

"No way. I'm never coming back here." She left Amore and I could hear her yelling down the cobblestone alley that I was not a real matchmaker. The would-be customers turned and walked away.

My heart raced.

A bad match.

I went into the kitchen to the walk-in refrigerator and stepped inside. I sat on the floor and held my head in my hands. A second later there was a knock on the door.

"What?" I called out to AJ.

A voice that wasn't AJ's asked, "Can I come in?"

Rico closed the door behind himself. "Bad day?" he asked, and sat down next to me.

"Pretty much."

"AJ filled me in. Was it the jalapeño?"

"No. It was mushroom and basil," I said. "You know, when I moved them together, I had a feeling it wasn't a good match."

"Then why did you do it?"

"Because to me, mushroom and basil just go together. Like peanut butter and jelly."

"Maybe you underestimate your gut."

I thought for a second. My gut was bubbling like a pot of simmering sauce at the moment. "Maybe I do."

We sat in silence for minute. "It's cold in here."

I didn't respond to the comment. "Maria, she used to be a matchmaker—"

"We went from zero matchmakers to two. Big week in Rome."

"And she made a bad match that made her feel so guilty that she stopped doing it." I explained Aunt Maria's story.

Rico asked, "Are you wondering if you should feel guilty?"

"The thought crossed my mind."

"I don't know what the Webster's Dictionary definition of matchmaker is, but I think you're just the thing that puts two people together. You create an opportunity to see if there is an initial spark," he said. "I don't think the matchmaker is in charge of everybody's happily ever after."

"Maybe," I said.

"That's the job of the fairy godmother."

That got a smile out of me. "It is?"

"Sure. They handle the whole bippity boppity boo." He asked, "Don't you guys get together for annual meetings or something?"

I chuckled.

"Well, you should."

"I guess we should," I said. "My notes, the ones about the matches, are missing. What am I gonna do about that?"

"I don't know, but we better find them before someone else does, or people all over Rome could be matching themselves based on pizza," he said. "That would be terrible. The city could crumble." He stood and held his hand out to help me up. When I stood, we were face-to-face.

His eyes.

I knew them.

I had definitely written about eyes exactly like his, or dreamed about them, or something. I had that déjà vu feeling again.

"Are you making fun of me?" I asked about Rome crumbling.

"Never," he said.

He opened the refrigerator door and let me leave first.

A loud burst of laughter came from the dining room. It was Jalapeño.

AJ fiddled with his phone while watching the dining room. "See." He pointed to my stomach. "Your gut did that."

Rico said, "Who needs notes?!"

Then AJ held up his phone. "You won't believe this."

"The post from that lady?" I asked, figuring the unsatisfied customer's words had jettisoned through the "interwebs" as Aunt Maria called it.

"No. I was flipping through FaceSpace to see what was going on, and guess what someone posted?" He didn't wait for us to answer. It says, 'Pizzeria Matchmaker's recipe for romance for sale.' And there's a photo." He showed me.

"Those are my notes!" I yelled.

"I guess we know what happened to them," Rico said.

I pointed to the background of the picture. It was a tiny silver corner of an old pinball machine. One I'd seen before.

"Oh no, he didn't," I said.

I picked up the broom and bopped the handle on the ceiling four times. Then I yelled up the vent, "Gianna Rossi, we need to talk!"

Four stomps followed, and a second later Gianna came in the back door. "What's up?" she asked.

AJ showed her the post.

"Oh my God. Are those your notes? You lost them?" she asked.

"No. I left them by the register, and now they're gone."

"Isn't that sort of the definition of lost?"

"Lost? They were *stolen*." I stared at her, waiting for her to catch on to my line of thought. "And I know by who."

"Who?" she asked. "You think *I* took them?"

"No. I think Lorenzo did." I pointed to the pinball machine. "Do you know where this picture was taken?"

She shook her head.

"At Pizzeria de Roma," I said.

She asked, "How do you know what Pizzeria de Roma looks like?"

Busted.

"That's not important. What we're talking about is that we heard Lorenzo and you talking through the vent the other night. Has he been back?"

"I haven't seen him since the spitball thing."

"I had my notes after that. How did he get them?"

"I don't know," Gianna said. "Maybe it wasn't him."

I looked at AJ's phone again. "People are bidding. It's up to eighty euros!"

Rico tapped numbers into his own cell phone. "Don't worry. I'm on it."

"What are you gonna do?"

He whispered, "I know a gu— Hey!" he said into the phone. "*Come stai, mio amico?*" He walked away so we couldn't hear him.

Just then our friendly neighborhood deliveryman came in, pushing a dolly stacked high with cardboard boxes. "*Buongiorno!*" he cried, the same way he had every other time he'd come into Amore Pizza. "Today I have butter and sugar and flour. Lots of flour." Vito spoke to him in Italian. I guess my Italian had improved, because I understood that Vito referred to our delivery guy as Salvatore and asked him about a man named Mossimo.

Salvatore asked Gianna, "Did you get the sample of the menu I left for you?"

"Yes. Thanks. I have just a few changes." Gianna went to the front of the store by the register to get the sample menu. She handed it to Salvatore.

He said, "I take it to the printer."

"Okay. Thanks," Gianna said.

I asked, "So you deliver everything?"

"I have a truck. I deliver anything anywhere. I used to run a restaurant myself, but I like to be out in the city. Not all day in the kitchen. So now I am silent partner. My brother and grandnephew, they run the restaurant. I do the accounting books at night, and all day I ride around and deliver stuff. Lots of sunshine."

"Which restaurant?" Gianna asked.

"Pizzeria de Roma. You know it. It is in the piazza by the Fontana del Cuore."

"Yeah," I said very casually. "I've seen it."

"I go now," Salvatore said. "*Ciao!*" he cried with his standard level of pep.

"*Ciao*," we echoed with much less excitement.

Once he was gone, I said, "He's Lorenzo's *great-uncle*."

"Seems that way," Rico said.

AJ asked, "Do you think he knows what Lorenzo did to the sauce and that he stole the matchmaker notes?"

"I don't know, but maybe Lorenzo will need to explain it to him when we give him a dose of his own medicine."

"Now?" Gianna asked.

"Tomorrow."

"What exactly is this master plan?" AJ asked.

I supplied the deets.

"I like the way your mind works," Rico said.

25

The next morning it was time to put my plan into motion. We walked through the piazza, past the Fontana del Cuore, and hid behind a statue near Pizzeria de Roma. Lorenzo's scooter wasn't out front. We waited for him to arrive and unlock the doors.

For this plan to work, Gianna was going to distract Lorenzo.

"Are you ready?" I asked her.

She chewed on her nails.

"Just like we practiced," Rico said. "You can do it."

Vroom!

"There he is," I said.

He parked his scooter, tucked his helmet under his arm, and headed for the door with keys in his hand.

"Now?" Gianna asked.

"Wait—wait—"

Lorenzo unlocked the doors and was just about to step inside when I said, "Now!"

Gianna walked toward Pizzeria de Roma with a hair flip, like we'd discussed, but—

Oh no!

The heel of her sandal caught between two cobble-stones, and she fell.

Epic fail.

"Ah!" she called out, getting Lorenzo's attention.

"Ouch." AJ winced. "That's gonna leave a mark."

"Not exactly like we rehearsed, huh?" Rico asked us.

"But it'll work," I said.

"Mamma mia!" Lorenzo left the door and hurried over to her. He bent down with his back to the door.

Gianna said, "I'm okay."

"Let me get you some ice," Lorenzo offered.

"Wait," she said to him. "Look at it. Do you think it needs a bandage, too?" She was improvising. I was proud of the improvement in her skills.

Perfect.

I tiptoed to the door and slid in, totally unnoticed.

I went down the hallway and entered the small office. I reached into my pocket and took out a paper bag filled with itching powder—something that Rico got from a guy who owned a joke shop.

I found the crisply ironed white uniform hanging on the back of the door and sprinkled the shirt and pants generously, especially in the butt region, if you know what I mean.

I went back to the front door and cracked it open to see if the coast was clear. Gianna still had Lorenzo perfectly distracted.

I dashed back behind the statue.

"Mission complete," I said to the guys.

"Roger that," AJ said.

Rico looked at us. "FBI? Secret agents?"

"I always wanted to write a story about a secret agent. Now I know how it feels."

Rico said, "Somehow I think secret agents are in a little more danger."

"Well," I said, "I just meant in general."

We watched as Gianna began to hobble to us with a napkin on her knee.

"Do you want me to bring you back to Amore?" Lorenzo asked her.

"No, thanks. I'll be okay."

"I'll see you tonight." He sounded genuinely sweet. "At the Festa."

She waved and he went inside.

When she was safely behind the statue, I asked, "Are you okay?"

She tossed the napkin in a nearby trash can and flipped her hair. *"Perfetto."*

She'd faked that fall?

Her skills had improved more than I'd thought.

26

"What do we do now?" AJ asked.

"Look through the windows and wait for the show," I said. "Then we complete phase two."

"There's a phase two?" Gianna asked.

"There's always a phase two," I assured her.

Lights inside Pizzeria de Roma came on, the hostess arrived, and just a short while later, customers walked in.

Through the windows we saw Lorenzo walk down the hall in his jeans and oxford shirt. A minute later he walked by wearing his white uniform.

"It won't be long now," I said.

Lorenzo walked to a table and talked to the customers. He rubbed at his collar.

More customers sat, and Lorenzo moved throughout the pizzeria. He began rubbing his shoulders, then his stomach, and finally his butt. And his butt some more.

We all laughed.

"It's perfect!" Rico said.

"Oh, I just don't want it to end," AJ said.

I looked at them. "Okay. It's time. I'm going back in."

"Good luck," they called to me as I scurried in, flew past the hostess, saying, "Sorry, I have to use the restroom," zipped down the hall and into the office, snatched Lorenzo's clothes off the floor, and ran back out.

I paused to see if the hostess was standing guard at the door, but she wasn't even there. She was in the dining room with her mouth hanging open, watching Lorenzo's spectacle. He wiggled and wriggled and danced from table to table, scratching every part of his body.

I laughed the entire way back to the statue.

AJ and Rico were rolling on the ground. "Itching powder is just so classic," Rico cried.

"You took his clothes?!" Gianna asked, surprised and maybe even angry.

I nodded while I laughed.

A second later Lorenzo hopped down the hallway toward the office.

"Oh, how I wish we could see what was happening now," I said.

Another minute later Lorenzo came out wrapped in a tablecloth toga. He got on his Vespa and took off with white flaps of cloth waving behind him like a cape.

27

Gianna braided my hair for the Festa. It was like a craft for her; she had a knack for it. I wore a supercute dress that I'd been saving for something special.

Gianna studied me in the mirror. "This is weird, but I think you look more grown-up than you did a week ago."

"Thanks." I looked at myself. She was right.

"What I want to know," Gianna said, "is which one do you like?"

"Which what?"

"Which guy? Rico or AJ?"

I hadn't thought about it that way. But I guess I wasn't thinking about *like* liking either of them. They were very different. And both of them were cute and fun to hang around with. "I don't know," I said.

"I think you like them both." She twirled a tendril of my hair that fell outside the braid.

"Which one should I like?"

"Isn't that *your* area of expertise? I do braids; you handle the romantic pairing." She turned to her own hair and began twisting it this way and that, sticking pins here and there.

"Are you totally bummed about Lorenzo?" I asked.

"Yeah, I am. He was really sweet to me," she said. "I guess some people are good at acting."

The piazza was decorated with streamers and lights. Each corner had live music of a different kind—violins, a mariachi band, steel drums, and a traditional rock band. Everywhere people danced in the street. It was like they'd never heard live music or danced before, and never would again.

Rico got us four Aranciatas and wedged through the crowd, looking for a place where we could stand. He took my hand and pulled me behind him through the crowd.

Did you hear the part where I said he was holding my hand?

Let me tell you what it was like. His skin was rougher and cool. I liked it—*like* liked it.

Rico and AJ turned out to be good dancers. The three of us clapped and sang in the night air.

I thought about how cool it was that in just a few days I'd made two great new friends. They were new friends, right? I was continually nagged by the thought that I'd met Rico before.

The night was fun, exciting, loud, and totally awesome sauce, except for Gianna. She wasn't joining in with us. When we took a short break to replenish our Aranciatas, I asked her, "What's up with you?"

"I'm feeling like that was pretty mean to do to Lorenzo. He's not even here. He probably can't get out of the shower."

"If I didn't think that he sabotaged the sauce and stole the notes, I might feel a little bad for him," I said. "But remember, he's messing with Aunt Maria. With Amore Pizzeria!"

Rico said, "No one messes with Maria."

AJ, Rico, and I tapped our soda bottles together.

"Yup," AJ said. "No one."

Gianna tapped her bottle to ours.

28

⁓

The next morning Aunt Maria took Meataball to get his claws trimmed, and I went to Amore. I was greeted by a handful of notes for the Pizzeria Matchmaker. The sound of Vito pounding chicken with a wooden mallet echoed off the exposed brick walls. The scraping work had been completed, and honestly, the place looked incredible. It was old-world and traditional, yet felt romantic and homey at the same time.

I lifted the humongous pot to a burner and started the ritual of making sauce, on my own, for the first time.

Even though we'd just made a batch, I wanted to try to do it myself.

I followed the directions the way I had memorized. Nothing was written down. And now I understood why. The oil bubbled, the garlic popped. Slowly I added the tomatoes a little at a time, stirring carefully with the very long silver spoon.

Going through the motions of mixing the steaming ingredients, with the rhythmic pounding in the background, allowed my thoughts to drift away in the steam floating from the pot. I wondered about:

1. AJ and Rico: Did I *like* like Rico or AJ? I thought the answer to this question was still "both." And what was it about Rico that made me want to stare at him and try to figure out where I thought I'd seen him before?
2. Letters: What was I going to do with these letters? Throwing away others' wishes seemed wrong. But the pile was getting big.
3. My notes: *Where were they now?*

The back door opened, followed by the familiar sound of "*Buongiorno!*" from the deliveryman named Salvatore. This guy seemed like he never had a bad day.

"Ah, you are making sauce," he said. "Maria taught you her recipe?"

"Yeah, she did," I said. "This is my first time flying solo."

"Really?" He moved closer to the pot and studied the empty jugs. "Where do you get your crushed tomatoes?"

"Can't tell you," I said. "It's a secret. You know that."

"Ha-ha!" His belly jiggled. "Everyone knows that. Between the sauce and the matchmaking thing, you guys are getting all the pizza customers."

"Yeah. I guess the matchmaking gets them in, and the sauce keeps them eating. A good combo," I said. "We wouldn't want to let those secrets out."

For the first time the perma-grin glued to Salvatore's face faded. The sudden change in his expression made the hairs on my neck stick up. Then, just as fast as it had disappeared, it returned, but this time it looked like he was forcing his face muscles to smile. It looked . . . *fake*.

Suddenly I didn't trust Salvatore.

The sauce—he was in the kitchen alone all the time.

The matchmaker notes—he'd delivered the menu sample near the register.

Did I make a terrible mistake?

I think I had.

Was I wrong about Lorenzo?

I think I had been.

29

"It was him," I said to Rico and AJ as soon as they had both feet in the kitchen. "He took my notes and put them up for an online auction."

"Not Lorenzo?" AJ asked.

"No," I said.

"So we—" Rico started saying.

"Yup," I said.

"And Lorenzo didn't—" AJ began.

"Nope," I said.

"Not cool," Rico said.

"Not at all," I confirmed.

"And why was he following us around Rome?" AJ asked.

"Maybe he was really following Gianna to talk to her," I suggested. "Like she thought."

"And we spit cherry seeds at him," Rico said. "Now I feel bad."

"Me too," I said.

"Why did Salvatore do it?" AJ asked.

"That is the one-million-pepperoni question," I said. "And we're gonna get an answer."

"How?" Rico asked.

"We're gonna go over there and ask. No more recon, no more acts of deception, no more stakeouts," I said. "AJ, can you stir this sauce for me?"

"Really? The sauce?" AJ asked.

"Yeah. Look, you have to do it like this." I showed him how to make big sweeping circles with the long silver spoon. "You can't stop." I handed it to him. "Ever."

"You're letting me use the spoon?"

"Yeah," I said. "I trust you."

He took the spoon and stirred it exactly like I had said.

I gave him a thumbs-up.

"You," I said to Rico. "You come with me."

I took Rico's hand and dragged him out the back door.

Did you get the part where I grabbed his hand?

I jumped on the back of his friend's Vespa, which Rico continued to borrow, and secured the helmet like a pro.

Rico took off with such speed that I had to grab him around the waist to keep myself from falling off. He zipped through the streets more aggressively than AJ had. I held on tight. He smelled good, like a familiar soap.

Again, I debated the question about which boy I *like* liked. Right now, it was Rico.

"We're going right in there and ask them why they're doing this to Amore Pizzeria." I set my helmet on the back of the scooter and marched toward the door. "You coming?"

"Um—"

"Wimp," I said.

He swung his leg off the scooter. "Wimp" did it.

I knocked on the back door of Pizzeria de Roma, hard. Lorenzo opened it.

"I need to talk to you," I said. I saw Salvatore and said to him, "And you."

"Come in," Lorenzo said.

The kitchen of Pizzeria de Roma was very different from Amore's. It was very big, bright, and filled with chefs with tall hats and shiny dishwashers. Every appliance shone and sparkled with newness.

"What's going on?" Lorenzo asked.

"That's my question." I looked at Salvatore. "And I think *he* can answer it."

"Uncle Sal?" Lorenzo asked.

Uncle Sal said nothing.

"He's been in Amore Pizzeria doing a little more than making deliveries, if you know what I mean. And I want to know why."

"No," Lorenzo said. "I don't know what you mean."

"I think he sabotaged our signature sauce with an insane, and potentially lethal, dose of red pepper. I tried it. I almost lost my tongue, literally. It almost fell right out of my mouth and onto the tile floor."

Lorenzo stared at Salvatore and then at his grandfather, who was also in the kitchen. "Did you ask him to do that?"

"I know nothing about this," Grandfather said. "What did you do, Salvatore?"

"I did what had to be done," Salvatore said. "You are blinded by *amore*. And that is going to kill our business. We will be broke."

"So, it is the truth?" Grandfather asked. "The sauce?"

Salvatore nodded. "First I look for the recipe for the sauce. But they no write it down. I look everywhere. It was the only thing keeping them open."

"But why?" Grandfather asked.

"We no make enough money to cover all of this." He pointed to the shining appliances. "With that sauce, people will eat more of our pizza."

"I hate to break it to you, but your pizza has more problems than the sauce, if you know what I mean," I said under my breath.

"The customers, they come once and no come back," Salvatore said. "Then they start with the matchmaking and we have no customers. When I see the matching instructions at the register—"

"What did you do with the instructions?" Lorenzo asked.

"He's selling them online. To the highest bidder," Rico said.

Lorenzo asked Uncle Sal, "So you were trying to put them out of business?"

"I have a lot of money invested in this place," Salvatore said. "It's my retirement. And you, Mossimo, you don't know how to run a restaurant."

Grandfather said, "Salvatore, I cannot believe what

you have done." To us, he said, "I am sorry. I would never want to hurt my dear Maria."

"Your . . . 'dear Maria'?" I asked slowly.

Everyone nodded.

"Yes," Grandfather said. "It is a very old story."

"Those are my favorite kind," I said. "Lay it on me." I hopped on the counter and made myself comfortable.

"It started when Maria and I were about your age."

"What happened?" Rico moved toward the cappuccino machine, pushed a few buttons, and rested a small white cup under a spout. "Does anyone else want one?"

Everyone nodded.

"She was so beautiful. We fell in love. But then I went into the military. We kept in touch for a long time with the letters. One day she write me that she was marrying Ferdinando. I was heartbroken and didn't write to her again."

Lorenzo helped Rico put tiny mugs into tiny saucers with tiny spoons and pass them around.

Grandfather continued his story as he stared at the wall. It was as if he was watching it play out on a movie screen and he was telling us what he saw.

"We lost the contact with each other. I thought I would never see her again. I married my dearest Nicolette. Loved her deeply. She died very young.

After two broken hearts, I never looked for the love again. A few months ago I decide to take money that I won from a national bocce tournament and move to Rome."

"He is very good at bocce," Lorenzo added. "And dancing."

Grandfather took a sip of espresso and continued, "I move here to Rome to be with my brother and his little restaurant. We make all the changes. Sal wanted a break from the cooking, so I take over and he start the deliveries. One day I visited the Fontana del Cuore. Like everyone, I toss in a coin. And that is when I saw her. At least I thought it was her. I could no be sure. It had been so many years. I followed her down a cobblestone alley to Amore Pizzeria, where she disappeared. I go in and order. When I try the pizza, I know the sauce. It was my Maria."

"What did you do?" I asked. At the same time I thought about how I was going to write a story about this when I got home.

"I left. I no talk to her."

He continued, "She is happily married and has a lovely life. I no want to interfere," he said.

"You know," I said, "Great-Uncle Ferdinando died three years ago."

"What?!" Grandfather said. He set his small espresso cup down and glared at Salvatore. "You knew this?"

"I—er—um . . ."

"You are every day making the deliveries. You knew?"

"*Sì!* I knew! If I told you, you would never try to make this business work!" he yelled. "When you came back that day and told me you'd found your true love at Amore Pizzeria, I would not believe it. In all the piazzas in all of Italy, and she owns a pizzeria *here*! What are the chances?"

"*Mamma mia!*" Grandfather smacked his forehead with his hand. "I cannot believe you no tell me, Salvatore." Suddenly he lunged at his brother.

I jumped in between them. "Wait!"

Lorenzo tried to calm his grandfather, while Rico subdued Salvatore.

"I have an idea," I said.

"Thank goodness," Rico sighed.

"I can't wait to hear this," Lorenzo said.

"By the way," I said to Lorenzo, "I am so sorry about the itching thing."

"That's okay," he said. "It's not like you had anything to do with—"

I stared at the floor.

"You? You did that? Why? I was nice to you and Gianna. I liked her. I still like her."

"I thought you had done it—the sauce, the notes."

I expected him to yell and get angry. Instead he combed his fingers through his hair. "No. It wasn't me."

His calmness made me feel worse, if that was even possible.

This story needed a much happier ending.

30

❧

I banged the broom on the ceiling. Jane came in with a big board covered with fabric.

"What's that?" I asked.

"It's a pin board. I'm going to make crisscrosses with ribbon. Then I'll slide pictures or memorabilia under the ribbons and make like a collage type of thing," she said. "Do you like it?"

"I do." This gave me *another* idea. They were coming faster than I could handle now.

"Guys, we need to have a little meeting."

I set myself at the head of a table for six. My sister and friends sat around me. Rico and I related the story about Aunt Maria and Grandfather Mossimo.

"What are we gonna do?" AJ asked.

"What we're good at," Gianna said. "Everyone is going to do what they're good at."

"I resisted my special skill because *someone*"—I eyed Gianna—"told me it was weird. But I'm matchmaking regardless of what people think."

"Obviously Maria is awesome at pizza," AJ said.

"Totes," I agreed. "Grandfather Mossimo—not so much. But he's got other skills he's not even using." To AJ I said, "And so do you." I looked at Rico. His expression said he wanted to hear what he was good at. "You have friends who owe you favors. We're gonna need them." To Jane I said, "I need a special dress made. Oh, and I'm gonna need that pin board thingy too."

"What about me?" Gianna asked.

"We're gonna need signs and flyers made," I said.

"I'm on it."

I laid out the details of my plan.

31

~~~~~~~~

The next day we mobilized the plan we'd created last night. I was on Aunt Maria duty.

"You know, Rico told me the story of Beatrice and Dante," I said as she and I made cannoli filling.

"Yes. You like?"

"I think the ending is sad. And I've been wondering, what do you think would've happened if they'd met again? You know, later, when they were older?"

"I think maybe a love like theirs would not have died. Some love is like that."

I asked, "Do you know a love like that?"

She pinched the dough together and didn't answer right away. "Sì. I have, but that was a very long time ago."

"What if you had a second chance at it?" I asked.

Aunt Maria gave me a curious look. Before she could respond, AJ stuck his bandannaed head through the opening between the dining room and kitchen. "Match needed at twelve o'clock."

I looked straight ahead—at the twelve o'clock position. No one was there. AJ didn't know what these positions meant. But it was cute that he tried. "Who?" I asked.

"The girls at table six."

Table six was not at the twelve o'clock position.

He'd sat the four girls who were in the other day. I remembered the girl with the mouth full of elaborate orthodontics. I thought her name was Riley, and I thought she was the one who was all about bacon. Her hair was pulled back in braids that were as pretty as the ones Gianna could make.

"Sorry," I said to Aunt Maria. "I'll be right back."

"Sì. You do the matching."

I approached the girls. "Hi there. Welcome back. So, how did the matches work out last time?"

The leader girl said, "I've been out with Evan three times. Your little pizza voodoo worked for me."

Another girl said, "I'm going out on a date with Ashton tonight."

"That's great," I said.

"But we're here to find a match for Riley," the leader said.

"Double bacon, right?"

She smiled. She was a very pretty girl.

"You're a tough one, because bacon is so unusual. I'll be back. Let me think for a minute." I strolled from table to table with a pitcher of water, refilling glasses and hoping I'd get a feeling from someone, but nothing stirred my gut.

That is, until I returned the pitcher back behind the counter to discuss the situation with AJ, who had made himself a big ol' slice of anchovy pizza.

Double bacon and anchovies?

I guess it made sense.

Maybe I hadn't seen it initially because I thought I *like* liked AJ myself.

What does a matchmaker do in a situation like this?

Anchovies didn't go with ham and pineapple.

I knew this.

My gut knew this.

Maybe I just liked him, not *like* liked him.

I said to him, "They asked for bread. And the girl

with the braids wanted an Aranciata. Can you bring those over to them?"

He folded the last quarter of his pizza into his mouth and, without swallowing, said, "Roger that."

I watched. They talked. Riley laughed at something AJ said. I took a cherry from a bowl in the kitchen and ate it, except for the pit, which I blew through a straw and shot at the leader girl.

Bing!

Hit her right in the forehead. She looked at me, and I waved for her to come over.

"What the heck?" she asked, annoyed.

"I need help right away with—with—with—the chocolate mousse pie. I can give you a free slice."

Her expression brightened. "I love chocolate."

Who doesn't?

"It's going to melt if it doesn't get eaten, like, right this second." I ran to the kitchen and got a half-eaten pie out of the refrigerator and put it on the counter with three forks. "Look at that," I said. "I only have three forks. Which of your friends do you think would want to help?"

Vito pushed a little bell, signaling an order was ready for pickup.

"That's probably Riley's double bacon. I'll bring it

170

to her. Bacon probably doesn't mix well with chocolate mousse pie. Am I right, or am I right?"

"I think you're right. I'll get the other girls," she said.

"Wait a sec," I said. I snatched the bacon pizza. "Would you give this to Riley? And this to AJ." I handed her an orange soda. "I have to get a lasagna out of the oven before it burns, if you know what I mean."

"Sure thing."

As I'd hoped, the three girls left Riley alone at the table and sat at the counter around the chocolate pie.

With three empty chairs now at the table, AJ sat. He started showing Riley pictures on his phone. The two of them didn't stop talking, and Riley laughed at pretty much everything AJ said.

It looked like another successful match! I was happy for AJ.

To the three girls devouring the chocolate mousse pie, I said, "I found another fork after all." I dug into the pie with them.

One of the girls pointed to the basket of letters for "Beatrice." "Can we look at those?"

"I guess so." I brought the basket over and took the empty cake plate away.

They unfolded them and read them to each other. "Can I tweet some of these?"

I said, "I guess that would be okay."

She took pictures of the notes and, with a click, sent them out into social cyberspace. A minute later her phone dinged—dinged—dinged.

"I'm getting tons of comments about these," she said. "You should start your own Instagram page with these. People love it."

It was a great idea.

"I'll tell you what," I said. "If you can do that for me, I'll hook you up with endless chocolate mousse pie for the next few days—for as long as I'm in Rome."

"Deal!" the girls squealed.

The three of them snapped pictures of the letters.

Then Lorenzo and Gianna came in through the front door. I looked back into the kitchen to see if Aunt Maria was watching. She still didn't like Lorenzo. Her back was turned as she shaped cannoli shells. "What's up, guys?" I asked.

Gianna said, "I came in to tell you that I'm taking the night off."

"Um—" I started, but she didn't wait for a response. They left holding hands as they walked down the cobblestone alley.

32

A few nights later, all the prep work for my plan had been completed. There was only one piece missing. I had my biggest—and most important—matchmaking challenge ahead of me.

"Aunt Maria," I said, "we're going out."

"Okay, Lucy. Have fun."

"No. You're coming too."

"Oh, no. I can't go out with you kids. You'll do all the games." She wiggled her fingers like she was holding a video-game controller. "And the computers." She panto-mimed a typing motion.

"Uh, kids usually don't work on computers when they go out," I said. "We're going to sing, dance, and play bocce!"

Aunt Maria clapped. "I love the bocce. I used to play a lot."

"I'll do your hair," Gianna said.

"Why? Is the place fancy?" Aunt Maria asked.

"No, we just thought it would be fun to dress up. And celebrate!" I said.

"What should I wear?" Aunt Maria asked.

Jane replied, "I have an idea."

On cue, Rico held up a flowery red dress.

"It's perfect," Gianna said.

"It will look great on you," AJ added.

"It is very *bellissima*," Aunt Maria said. "How can I say no?"

"You can't," I said. "Get ready."

We all walked together into the piazza, which looked different now. The colorful sign for Pizzeria de Roma had been replaced with a DANZA ITALIANO sign.

"What is this?"

"Surprise! It's not a pizzeria anymore," I said.

AJ explained, "They have dancing and singing and indoor bocce."

We went inside and saw Lorenzo standing at the podium. "Your table is waiting for you," he said.

We followed Lorenzo to a large round table close to the stage. The lights had been dimmed, the music turned up. AJ didn't even sit down. He walked to the stage and pressed a few buttons on a big piece of stereo equipment—which I guess was kind of video gamey and computerish—and a second later the beat of a popular dance song came on.

Then AJ started singing. *That's* what he was good at.

Okay, so I'll tell you about his karaoke. It wasn't terrible, but he was far from good. It didn't seem to matter, because people of all ages jumped to the dance floor. Even Aunt Maria left her Aranciata on the table and danced. That is, before she froze.

She looked like she'd seen a ghost.

"*Mamma mia!*" she said. "Is that you?"

"Yes," Mossimo said.

She walked up to him, and they hugged. A tear rolled down Aunt Maria's cheek.

Mossimo wiped it off. "I've thought about seeing you again for a very long time," he said. "You look exactly the same."

"Um," I said to Rico. "How about a game of bocce?" I had never actually played the game, but I wanted to give

175

Aunt Maria some privacy. Rico and I challenged AJ and his new "friend" Riley.

Mossimo led Aunt Maria to a small table in the back corner. I spied as they looked into each other's eyes and talked.

I hadn't been a matchmaker for very long, but if this was what it felt like, I wanted to do it forever. I was so happy to have helped them find each other again—and write the perfect ending to their story.

33

Pizzeria de Roma's transformation to a singing, dancing bocce club was a huge success. All the pizza lovers in the piazza now came to Amore to eat, then went to Danza Italiano to have fun. AJ's new friend Riley and her three social-media-maven girlfriends maintained our website and also got jobs at the pizzeria for the rest of the summer. Rico and his friends had set up tables and chairs outside so we could offer dining alfresco.

The first order I took a few nights later was from Murielle duPluie and Angelo.

"*Bonjour,*" she said.

"Hi!" I was excited to see her.

"I am going to do the follow-up article we talked about," she said. "And have dinner with *mon amour* at the same time."

"Great." To Angelo I said, "Nice to see you again."

"The place looks different," said Angelo in perfect English. "I love the outside seating and new menu."

"Thanks."

"I just *adore* the walls," Murielle duPluie said. "The exposed brick is *très jolie.*" The paint had been scraped from the rest of the bricks and the walls really did look great.

I took their order and was about to leave when Carina, the lady selling flowers who I'd met on the Spanish Steps, walked by with her basket. "Flower for the lady?" she asked Angelo.

"Of course," Angelo said. "I'll take two." He gave one of them to me and the other to Murielle duPluie.

"*Grazie,*" I said, and walked away with Carina. I asked her, "I'm just wondering, what did Aunt Maria do for you that you would do anything for her?"

"She introduced me to my husband." She smiled and offered roses to two more customers.

Ha. Even when Aunt Maria had stopped officially matchmaking and was "no messing with the love," she'd still managed to create some very happy couples on the sly.

AJ called to me from the kitchen, "You have a phone call at twelve o'clock."

I looked straight ahead.

The only thing there was the men's room.

"No. Sorry. I meant right here." He held up the phone.

Who would be calling me at Amore Pizzeria?

"Hello," I said.

"Hi, honey."

"Hi, Dad. I'm kinda busy right now."

"I know. I just wanted to tell you that Mom and I are reading all these letters on the website and looking at the pictures of Amore Pizzeria. It's just incredible."

"Thanks. There's actually a lot more I can tell you. Like Aunt Maria reconnecting with her Dante, whose name is Mossimo, and the menu and the dance club, but I've got a lot of hungry people here who need me to match them."

There was a long pause. Finally Dad said, "Okay, honey. I didn't understand all that, but I wanted to tell you how proud we are of you."

"Thanks, Dad. Bye—"

"Lucy! Wait."

"What?"

"I was wondering if you ever met Enrique. He used to hang around the shop."

"Who's that?"

"A boy you were friends with last time we went to Italy. You were in, like, first grade then."

"I don't remember any boy."

"Sure you do," my dad said. "He's in your stories. You call him something different every time, but I recognize him."

I knew the character Dad was talking about, but I didn't know anyone named Enrique.

"No, Dad, I haven't seen him."

"Too bad. You were pals back then," he said. "I'll see you at the airport tomorrow night, honey."

I hung up.

I finished the dinner crowd, wondering if I had a Dante of my own and didn't even realize it.

How would I find him in a huge foreign city like Rome?

Vito tapped my shoulder and pointed to several take-out tins of food filled with pizzas and spaghetti Parmesan sandwiches. He chattered something in Italian. I understood that he wanted me to deliver that stuff to Rico, who was in charge of the Amore Pizzeria mobile cart, which sold food in the piazza. It had a huge Amore Pizzeria sign and an arrow pointing down the alley.

I took the warm tins toward Rico. On my way I passed the Fontana del Cuore. I set the tins on the ground, reached into my pocket, found a coin, and tossed it in. I closed my eyes and thought—*Enrique*.

180

When I opened my eyes, Enrique hadn't miraculously appeared, so I took the tins to the cart, which was manned by Rico and one of his buddies.

"Who's hungry?" I asked.

"Actually," he said, "I'm starving. Do you want to take a break and chow with me?"

I untied my apron. "Yup. I absolutely would."

He asked, "What can I get for you?"

"Spaghetti Parmesan sandwich," I said. "I hear they're fabulous."

"If there was a zombie apocalypse and all we had were spaghetti Parm sandwiches, we would never have to worry about zombies wanting to eat brains. They would be totally satisfied with these." He handed me a warm sandwich wrapped in foil.

Had he seriously just referenced a zombie apocalypse?

"What are you going to have?" I asked him.

"Duh. My favorite. I haven't been able to get it anywhere. Until now, that is. You added it to the new menu." He held out a plate of ham-and-pineapple pizza. "The Los Angeles."

Did you get the part where I said Rico's favorite pizza was ham and pineapple?

That's my favorite too, and best matched with *another* ham and pineapple, generally speaking. Of course, it isn't an exact science. I use my gut, too. And right now my gut was tangled like linguine al dente being dumped into a colander.

"When my parents decided to move back here from the US, I was homesick for my American friends. Then I met an American girl here on vacation. She introduced me to it, and ever since then it's been my numero uno favorite."

"As a kid? An American?"

"Yeah. She was on vacation here in Rome and I met her. We hung out for a week and then she was gone. I never saw her again." He bit into the pie. "But she left me with ham and pineapple."

"Enrique?"

Rico made a face. "Oh man, I hate that name. Don't call me that. Rico is much more fitting to my personality, don't you think?"

"Totes." He didn't put it together that I was the American girl, and I didn't tell him. At least not yet.

This was going to make a great story someday.

Then it happened.

Rico reached into his back pocket and took out my matchmaking notes. "I won the auction," he said, and gave them to me. Then he took me by the hand. We walked down the cobblestone alley—which was now lined on either side by glowing luminaries—with Meataball waddling behind us.

Can one girl find luck and
adventure on the Emerald Isle?
Read on for a peek at
Lost in Ireland
by Cindy Callaghan.

Previously titled *Lucky Me*

1

If I had to pick one thing that I believe in more than anything else, it would be this: LUCK. I'm Meghan McGlinchey, the most superstitious thirteen-year-old girl in Delaware, and possibly the world.

For example, I never got out of bed when my digital clock read an odd number. Odd number = bad luck.

7:02. Perfect.

I dressed in a snap because every day it was the same school uniform—boring plaid skirt, plain white shirt, itchy button-up navy-blue sweater, matching headband, horrendous blue leather shoes, and kneesocks. The outfit was— how should I say this?—ugly!

I dashed down the stairs, especially careful to skip

the thirteenth step today because it was a very important day, one I'd been looking forward to for weeks. I was running for eighth-grade class president. And today was the election. I had done a stellar job campaigning FOREVER. If I didn't totally mess up my speech, I was pretty sure I was gonna win. With all the practicing I'd been doing, it would take a major freak of nature for me to mess it up.

I passed my four sisters and parents scrambling around in the kitchen. I opened a can of food for my cat, Lucky. He ran over when he heard it pop. I scratched his ears as he lapped up the food.

I loved Lucky, but he and I had a problem. He was a black cat. And people like me, we didn't mix well with black cats. But we had an understanding: He didn't cross my path, and I took good care of him. It worked for us.

The kitchen was louder than usual this morning. My younger sister Piper (the fifth grader) yelled at one of my older sisters, Eryn (the eleventh grader), "Why did you touch my playlist? Why? WHY?"

Dad yelled across the kitchen to my mom, "Can you put a bagel in the toaster for me?"

The baby, Hope, cried while my oldest sister sang her

an Irish lullaby to calm her. It wasn't working, so she tried some applesauce, which the baby threw across the room. It nearly hit my white shirt, but I ducked out of the way just in time. *SPLAT!* The applesauce hit the wall behind me.

Phew, that was lucky!

I stood at the front door, under the horseshoe mounted on the wall and next to my snow globe collection, watching the insanity.

The living room was a mess with suitcases and duffel bags. We were leaving the next morning for Ireland, where we would spend spring break. The purpose of the trip was for my father to meet his newly discovered sister. You see, he'd been born in Ireland. Sadly, something happened to his parents when he was just a kid, and he'd been raised at a home for boys.

Until a few months ago he hadn't thought he had any family. But thanks to some online research, he'd found a long-lost sister. I imagined that when he met her, he'd introduce me as his middle daughter and president of Wilmington Prep's eighth-grade class. It was gonna be totally impressive.

I crunched the granola bar I'd packed in my back-pack the night before—instant breakfast. With a little planning, my morning was the way I liked it: mayhem-free.

In fact, I liked most things organized. I might have been the most organized eighth grader at Wilmington Prep, an all-girls private school that went from kindergarten through twelfth grade. This meant that Piper and Eryn were in my school. If you knew either Piper or Eryn, you'd know this wasn't a good thing. (Piper was known as the bigmouth, while Eryn was quiet and filled with a bad attitude. I'd heard a lot of nicknames for her, most made up by my bestie, Carissa. None of them were nice.)

While I waited for someone to realize it was time to leave, I flipped through a Forever 21 catalog.

"Meghan," Mom called through the chaos. "You have a letter on the table."

"A letter?" I asked.

"Yes," she said. "You know, the regular old-fashioned paper kind that's delivered by a mailman."

I stepped around the chaos. Sure enough, on the hall table was a letter addressed to *moi*.

Who writes letters anymore when you can just text or e-mail? The postmark on the envelope said Limerick, Ireland. *Hmmm.*

Dear Friend,

I am starting this chain letter and mailing it to three people to whom I would like to send good luck. In turn they must send it to three people. If you are receiving this, someone has sent the luck to you—as long as you, in turn, send it to three more people within six days.

Chain letters have existed for centuries, and many have traveled around the world. A United States police officer received $25,000 within one day of sending his letters. However, another woman ignored it and lost her life's fortune because she broke the chain. A Norwegian fisherman thought for sure he would never find true love, but just two days after sending his letters, he met the woman of his dreams.

To get your luck and avoid the unlucky consequences, you must:
- Copy this letter
- Add your name below and remove the name above yours
- Mail it to three people within <u>six</u> days

From,

4. <u>Clare Gallagher, Ireland</u>

5. _____

Clare Gallagher?

I didn't know anyone by that name. *How does she know me?* That wasn't important now. What *was* important was that I send this letter to three people ASAP. No, double-ASAP. Maybe I could get the good luck as soon as today—for the election—and avoid those "unlucky consequences."

I went into my mom and dad's home office and rummaged around.

"What are you doing in there?" Mom called over the havoc.

"Looking for envelopes!"

"I don't have any," Mom said. "Sorry. I'll bring a few home from work tonight."

That would be too late. Maybe I could get a couple from the school office. I only needed three. "How about stamps?"

"Sorry. The baby used them as stickers. I can buy more after vacation."

After vacation wasn't *today*, and I needed the luck *today*.

Eryn bumped me out of her way, causing me to drop the letter. "Move it, buttmunch," she said. She stepped on the letter as she left the house. (This is what I meant about her attitude—bad.)

Piper did pretty much the same thing on her way out, not because she had attitude issues but because she wasn't paying attention.

Shannon picked the letter up for me. She was twenty-two years old and definitely the nicest of my sisters. She commuted to the University of Delaware, and itched to finish school so she could move out of our house and "find herself," whatever that meant.

I took the letter, followed Shannon to the car, and climbed into the back with Piper. Eryn sat shotgun. Always. I didn't even try to beat her to the front seat anymore. Shannon always dropped us off at Wilmington Prep, then headed to UD. She picked us up later, on her way home. After school, we did homework or whatever until Mom or Dad got home from the law firm where they worked together. They were always home for a late full-family dinner, when we talked about our day, whether we wanted to or not.

On our drive Piper chattered about our spring break trip, while I just stared out the window.

"What do you guys know about chain letters?" I asked.

Shannon said, "You need to send 'em right away, don't you?"

I could feel Eryn rolling her eyes.

Piper asked a hundred questions: "What's a chain let-ter? . . . Who sent it? . . . Why? Can you send it back? . . . Why not? How come I didn't get one? . . . Huh?"

I didn't answer her; I responded to Shannon. "I don't have any stamps or envelopes, and I want the good luck today."

"Why don't you e-mail it?" Shannon asked. "You could do that right now on your phone."

Piper said, "Problem solved. Shannon is supersmart. . . ." She continued to ramble on while I typed the letter quickly with my thumbs. I reread it to make sure I hadn't made any mistakes. I put my name on the bottom and didn't put Clare's. When I finished, Piper was still talking. "She gets As in college. That's a lot of hard work."

I hit the send button on my phone, and e-mail chain letters went out to three friends from summer camp. "Okay. It's done. Let the good luck begin!"

Eryn snickered.

"What?" I asked.

"Oh, nothing," she said with a smirk. "Let me know how that works for you. On second thought, don't. That would mean you'd be talking to me." She made a grossed-out face that I caught in the side mirror. "But any moron knows that you can't e-mail a snail-mail chain letter. It's cheating. And chain letters have a way of messing with cheaters."

Piper said, "Uh-oh."

Uh-oh?

I couldn't have any *uh-oh.*

Not today.

2

As soon as I walked into science class, it looked like Eryn might have been right. "Miss McGlinchey," Ms. Geneva called to me. "Please report to the front of the classroom for a demerit."

A *demerit?* I didn't get demerits. I followed all the rules all the time, to avoid getting demerits. I followed the rules even when demerits *weren't* involved. I flossed, waited twenty minutes after eating to swim, and wore SPF 50 sunscreen every day.

I took the yellow paper from her hand. For each demerit you got, you missed one recess. If you got five, you were suspended from school for a day. Ms. Geneva must have read the puzzled look on my face. She gestured toward my feet. "Your socks."

I looked down. One black, one blue.

OMG! Somehow, for the first time in my history of wearing kneesocks, I had accidentally mismatched them. *But that could happen to anyone, right?*

I sulked all the way back to my desk.

"What the heck?" Carissa looked shocked as I sat back down.

"My stupid socks don't match," I grumbled.

Carissa chuckled. "You can hardly tell," she said a little bit too loudly.

"Shh," I said. "Or you'll get one too."

"Oh, like that would be something new. You know they named a desk after me in detention. Not many people can claim that." Carissa missed a lot of recesses, and she'd been suspended twice. On those days, she said she'd sat on the couch all day eating popcorn and watching on-demand movies—R-rated. Her mom was home way more than mine but never had a clue what Carissa did. Carissa's life was kinda the opposite of mine.

The teacher said, *"Mademoiselle Carissa Lyons, fermez la bouche!"* Everyone has to take French as part of Wilmington Prep's curriculum, so we both knew that was a teacher's polite way of saying "Shut up."

. . .

Considering all the preparation I'd done, I was way more nervous for my speech than I should've been. I sat on the stage, in mismatched socks, in front of the entire eighth-grade class. This speech would seal the election for me. I'd worked hard on it, and it was—how can I say this so that it doesn't sound like I'm bragging?—perfect! I had nothing to worry about.

I imagined the scene as though it was frozen in one of my lucky snow globes: I'm on stage delivering my last sentence, but before I finish, the room booms with applause. Kids stand up and cheer. My opponent is so intimidated, she walks offstage—she doesn't stand a chance. She knows it. I know it.

The principal introduced me and my opponent, Avery Brown, and she explained that we each had four minutes.

I was up first. I stepped to the podium and began:

"Fellow classmates," I started confidently, "my name is Meghan McGlinchey. I want to be your class president for three very important reasons. First, I am filled with Wilmington Prep school spirit. . . ."

I looked into the crowd and noticed that everyone was talking to each other like I wasn't even there.

I held up two fingers. "Secondly." Still the crowd talked among themselves. I could hear them like a rumble. Why weren't they listening to my amazing speech? I was being very clear, articulate, and was holding up fingers.

Principal Jackson came out from behind the stage's curtain and walked over to the podium, where I was already talking about point number three and holding up three fingers.

"Excuse me," she whispered, interrupting my flow.

I whispered back to her, "What's the matter?"

"The microphone—" She flipped a switch with her thumb, and her words bellowed: "IT ISN'T TURNED ON!" She moved it away from her mouth. "It is now."

My fellow classmates laughed.

They hadn't heard a single perfect word I'd said. I started over. "My name is—"

The girl who was keeping time in the front row said, "One minute."

One minute?

"Reason number one . . ." I raced.

"Number two . . ." I spoke faster, threw up two fingers.

"And number three—"

"Time!" the timekeeper said.

Principal Jackson walked out clapping her hands. "Thank you, Meghan."

"B-but," I sputtered. "The mic."

"Very good job. Next we have Avery Brown."

I passed Avery as I went back to my chair and she approached the podium. She said, "Bad luck for you."

It was.

What have I done?